ATLANTA FISH FRY

Life's a Fish and Then You Fry

ANTHONY "AJ" JOINER

STERLING & STONE

ATLANTA FISH FRY

Prologue
_____

THEY SAY the only constant in life is change. I've never really believed that. Change is the passage of time, the aging of bodies, the movements of fish as their schools swim through the sea.

But the constants are the things you hold onto, the things that ground you and give you something to cling to when evolution comes howling around you. Something that reminds you of who you are.

Your constants might be the love in your life, the people you care about, or the simple traditions that remind you that you're part of something bigger than yourself. The people that came before you passed through a lifetime of change by holding onto those touchpoints that mattered most.

And they passed those touchpoints on to you.

What's my touchpoint?

That's easy ... Fish Fry Day.

Twenty years ago ...

Little Anthony looked over at Jamal, wishing he could do some of the same manly things that his burly uncle could do, before reminding himself — like Mom and Grandmoh were always doing — that one day he too could do whatever he wanted. Everyone was always telling him to be patient, but that was like asking a fish not to swim.

And it wasn't like Anthony was always impatient. Fish Fry Day was about the good things finally coming to those who wait, with his excitement beating the dawn and the burgeoning thrill lasting until the last full belly finally staggered home. Today shouldn't be any different. Right now, Anthony was clutching a string of chicken guts for bait, standing waist-deep in murky water with Jamal. But soon, they would be heading back home with whatever they managed to catch so they could process all that fish with Grandmoh, seeing as she'd been awaiting their haul since before the boys had even left.

Anthony was always excited when it came time for another fish fry. And though he was still thrilled, today was different. He usually loved every moment, from setup to cleanup. But today was tainted by the unthinkable thing he couldn't stop thinking about.

"You doing okay there, kid?" Jamal asked him.

He nodded and smiled. The wrong answer might lead his well-intentioned uncle to questions that Anthony didn't want to think about, let alone answer. "I'm good."

"Someone should tell your face." His uncle laughed. "Almost looks like you forgot what day it was."

Anthony didn't respond.

"What day is it?" Jamal asked.

Anthony told himself to stop thinking about the thing he didn't want to think about, at least long enough to let a tiny smile creep onto the corner of his mouth. Then he finally said, "It's Fish Fry Day."

Jamal twisted his face into a knot of confusion, then

put a hand to his ear. "I'm sorry, little man, but I couldn't hear a word you just said."

Anthony smiled wider. "IT'S FISH FRY DAY!"

"Much better."

Jamal laughed as Anthony felt a tug on his chicken guts. "I got something!"

"Of course you do." Another hearty laugh from his uncle as he slapped a large hand on Anthony's bony shoulder. "You always got something."

Several hours later, they were back home and in the middle of what should have been the best fish fry of Anthony's life so far. Instead, he was still doing his best to ignore the unthinkable thing, regardless of how hard and how often it kept knocking on his mental door. Disregarding those thoughts should have been simple enough, considering the bounty of happy commotion all around him.

Grandmoh lived in a little house on a small street that barely seemed to be winning its war against an aggressive belt of Louisiana nature closing in to reclaim it. But size didn't matter when it came to her fish fries. The narrow road was littered with kids, most of them running around and playing games on the asphalt while the grownups boogied to music that could probably be heard all the way over in Mississippi.

Anthony looked around at all the fish and the food and the laughing and dancing and told himself for what had to be the hundredth, or perhaps even the millionth time that week: he needed to enjoy what was right in front of him instead of fixating on what wasn't. Just like Mom and Grandmoh, and probably Uncle Jamal and everyone else in his whole life kept telling him to.

The table around Anthony filled with familiar faces:

Old Aunty Eileen with her cheeks cratered and cracked with laugh lines, Mom and Grandmoh seated side-by-side looking like a before and after photo, and even his sometimes favorite cousin and occasional worst enemy Michael whose nose was smeared with brown seasoning.

Anthony loaded his plate with another pile of fish and an extra-large helping of coleslaw, then he turned to Grandmoh with a smile wide enough to use it again on Santa come December. "How come the church fish fry never tastes as good as yours?"

Grandmoh grinned, humble but proud. "Spice a dish with love and it pleases every palate."

"But the church is all about love," Anthony argued.

"Well, you're right about that." Grandmoh laughed. "In that case, I don't mind telling you that the secret is Tony Chachere's Fish Fry Seasoning."

"But the church uses that, too. I've seen it myself."

"Sure they do, just not enough of it."

"How much is enough?"

"Approximately one shake before it's too much." Grandmoh laughed again.

Best to leave it at that. Anthony swallowed and shoved another giant bite into his mouth, hoping the eating would outrun his stomach. He had developed a simple system to optimize the potential deliciousness of each and every fish fry: eat as much as he possibly could, as fast as he possibly could, then hang out with his cousins as his food slowly settled. Not enough for him to get hungry again, but definitely enough for him to enjoy a slice or two of peach cobbler.

The cards came out as plates were cleared. Grandmoh was the queen of whist, but it seemed to Anthony that was more because she was the only one paying attention rather than being due to any inherent skill. Everyone else was busy leaning back and unbuttoning belts to care much about their cards. Anthony had to try not to look at them, the reminder that the Fish Fry Day was drawing to a close, and so much more would be ending with it.

He looked around for a way to distract himself and spotted a gaggle of kids quarreling over the last boiled crawfish. Two minutes later, Anthony was holding court for his wild-eyed cousins, spinning a mostly true yarn about the catfish he'd caught with Uncle Jamal while music from Down in the Treme played in the background.

"You're full of it," said Michael, younger than Anthony but still old enough to doubt his cousin's story.

"Am not."

"How come you don't have no mark on your arm if the catfish bit you?" Michael asked.

Anthony looked down at his arm, disappointed to see that his bite marks had already faded … not that they were all that deep to begin with.

"I guess they went away." He shrugged. "That don't mean it didn't happen."

Ada looked over in disbelief. "You really just stuck your arm into an underwater cave without knowing what all might be in there?"

"Uncle Jamal went first," Anthony explained. "So I knew it was fine."

Little Jade said, "How come there's no catfish to eat if you all caught one?"

"Because we let it go." Anthony hoped his authoritative tone would make it harder for his cousins to question him.

"Sure you did." Michael clearly didn't believe him. "But even though your pants are on fire about catching that catfish, I'll still let you have one of my mom's French fries."

He held out the plate in offering. Anthony was still too

full, and needing room for his cobbler, but he wasn't about to lose face in front of his most obnoxious cousin. So he reached over, casually grabbed a fry, and shoved it into his mouth.

But it wasn't a French fry.

It was a hot pepper with pure hell packed tightly inside it.

"I NEED MILK!" Anthony roared at Mom as he ran from the table, ignoring the chorus of laughter behind him, obnoxiously clanging from his cousins with Michael in the lead like always.

Anthony drank his milk as time seemed to speed up around him. The women cleaning and laughing together, the men closing up the fryers and reaching for those final pieces of cobbler. Soon all but Grandmoh's table had been moved to the side, and the real dancing had begun. Normally Anthony would be right out there with them, but the unthinkable thing had become all he could think about. So he sat quietly next to Grandmoh, holding firm to her wrinkled hand.

"So, Geraldine, what's next?" asked Aunty Eileen, sitting on the far end of the table. "I imagine you've been waiting on this for a while?"

Uncle Joe spoke before Grandmoh could answer. "It's a shame that this will be the last one of your fish fries. We're sure gonna miss this place."

There. The unthinkable had been said out loud, and all the sorrow seemed to flood into Anthony at once.

There wasn't enough space in his stomach for all of the food in there already, same as there wasn't enough room in his head for all those uncomfortable thoughts.

"I'll miss it too, but—"

"YOUR FISH FRIES ARE THE BEST IN THE

WORLD!" Anthony blurted before Grandmoh could finish her thought.

Then he scampered up and away from the table.

By the time the sun was finally setting, Anthony could no longer ignore the ugly truth that had been scratching at his brain all day: it wasn't just this fish fry that would be going away; it was all of them. Forever.

So he locked himself in the bathroom and refused to come out.

"Anthony ..." Mom knocked again. "It's time."

But Anthony didn't respond.

This was her third attempt in five minutes. Anthony was pushing it, of course, but he didn't know what else to do. Barricading himself inside the bathroom forever meant never saying goodbye. Not to this place, nor to the Louisiana tradition he'd loved for longer than he could remember.

"Your brother and sister are waiting in the car."

Anthony heard her sigh from the other side of the door when he still didn't respond, then suffered several long moments of anxious silence before he heard another, softer knock on the door.

"Anthony?" Grandmoh said. "Do you mind if I come in?"

Keeping the door closed when Mom asked him to open it up was hard, but refusing his grandmother in her own house felt downright impossible.

Anthony opened the door, then she slipped inside and closed it behind her.

He had at least a bajillion things to say, but he burst into tears before he could get even one of them out.

"It's okay, honey ..." Grandmoh hugged him close.

"I don't want you to go!" Anthony continued to weep.

7

"I know, sweetheart …" She pulled him tighter, patting the back of his head.

"I love it here … and I love your fish fries … and I …"

He couldn't finish another sentence, and Grandmoh didn't make him. Instead, she held him against her until Anthony finally stopped crying.

Then she crouched down, took both of his hands, and looked right into her grandson's eyes. "We can't wish change away. If you're not growing, that means you're dying, and I'm much too old to start dying now." Grandmoh gave him a smile and squeezed his hands even tighter. "Nothing can last forever, and if it did, then don't you think life would be awfully boring?"

Anthony had never thought about it like that, but now he was listening.

"What do you love most about the fish fries?" Grandmoh asked.

"Everything," he answered because that was the truth.

"By 'everything,' do you mean the food and the feelings and the family?"

He nodded, knowing that trying to make words would get him crying again.

"Well, you won't always be in the places you love most, but you can be responsible for creating all those feelings of family and home wherever you go."

"What does that mean?" Anthony asked.

Grandmoh was wise, so he knew that her next words would stay with him even longer than the cobbler.

"It means nothing lasts forever, but home is where you make it."

Chapter One

ANTHONY OPENED his eyes to a new day ... and a fierce ringing in his head.

He knew from some unfortunate recent experience that the incessant throbbing would turn into a more complicated, compounding headache if he was lucky and a migraine if he wasn't careful.

Not that caution had anything to do with it.

He'd refused Kevin's insistent invitation to go out drinking with him last night, which would have saved his coworker from attending another workplace get-together alone. Anthony thought the outing sounded about as much fun as the average pile of homework. Instead, he'd watched a movie with Renee and gone to bed early. So this was just another one of his semi-regular headaches and not a hangover.

But the headaches were becoming more frequent. They had been hitting him hard (and sometimes harder) for a few months now. He squinted and pinched the bridge of his nose when they came, according to Renee. An involuntary action, but that didn't stop her from noticing. Renee always noticed everything.

She was already out of bed, probably running. But he could smell the coffee, and the aroma in his nostrils got his mouth watering.

He threw off the covers and planted his feet on the floor, squinting as he pinched the bridge of his nose on his way to the bathroom.

Renee liked making him coffee, and he liked making her breakfast. A few minutes later, he was sipping piping hot brew from a freshly poured mug of Kenyan from the French press and cracking a half-dozen eggs into his grand-moh's ancient skillet — the same one she used to flash fry some of his favorite childhood memories.

His timing was practically perfect — by the time Anthony was sitting at their small table and stabbing his fork into a steaming scrambler while staring out the window, the front door was slamming closed.

"What are you looking at this time?" Renee asked, back from her run.

"Wendall and Ezekiel." Anthony didn't turn to look, but he could hear the smile in her voice. "They're having some sort of argument."

"Again?"

"Sure looks that way." Anthony laughed.

Wendall Patterson was several courses short of a banquet and could often be found wandering aimlessly downtown, wearing his sandwich board like a T-shirt while loudly declaring that not only was the end in fact nigh but that the world's sinners — Atlanta had an abundance, according to Wendall — would all be going to Hell when it happened.

Anthony and Renee were new to the cul-de-sac but still assumed their neighborly duty, same as everyone else did, as assigned by Mrs. Jones. If anyone on Edgewood Street ever saw Wendall out and about, downtown or otherwise, they were supposed to help him get back home and, depending on who found him, maybe even offer the old guy a meal.

Nutty as Wendall was, his son was even nuttier.

"What are they arguing about?" Renee asked.

"Not sure." Anthony shrugged. "It just started, and my lip-reading isn't what it used to be."

"What did it used to be?"

He hid his smile behind his coffee mug. It didn't used to be anything. Anthony had never effectively read a pair of lips in his life. Not that he was above constantly trying. But it didn't matter if he was lip illiterate, seeing as he was perfectly capable of making up his own damn story.

"It looks like Wendall is mad at Ezekiel for failing to understand that the four horsemen of the apocalypse are galloping right toward Atlanta without even stopping for water, and Ezekiel is pissed that his old man won't board his brand new rocket to Mars."

"How long do you think we'll need to be married before I can finally get a straight answer out of you?" Renee asked.

"I love all of your curves so much, I was hoping you might love some of mine."

Renee laughed as she scooped the remaining scrambler from Grandmoh's skillet onto her plate, then came over and sat across from him, sharing his view out the window.

The quarrel on the street was warming between Ezekiel and Wendall — father and son both had their hands raised, their voices loud as they barked at one another. The pair was far enough down the cul-de-sac to mute their heated exchange. That was fine. Anthony could ask Rob and Riley for details later if he really wanted to know. Their favorite neighbors enjoyed watching the Wendall and Ezekiel Experience almost as much as he did.

Renee shook her head. "Sorry my aunt's house is surrounded by nut jobs."

"Nut jobs are people too." Anthony laughed. "Besides, do you really think I want to live in some boring-ass neighborhood filled with boring-ass people? I've always loved a good story."

"You're definitely full of them."

"All true, I promise." He winked at Renee.

"I'm sure it would have been nice to live in a place where—"

"Baby." He dropped his fork and stared into her big brown eyes. "How many times do I have to say the same things before you finally start to believe me?"

She shrugged. "Of course, I appreciate how much you say you're happy with this house and the neighborhood … but sometimes you're too optimistic and—"

"*Too optimistic*? Is there such a thing?"

"Anthony …" Renee laughed. "You're always so sure the glass is half full that you don't even realize when we've run out of water."

That one stung a bit, but he chuckled like it didn't. "This is the right place for us. All of the other places weren't just more expensive than taking your aunt up on her offer; they were soulless."

"That seems a bit harsh."

"I don't need a Starbucks on the corner or a specially marked 'green space.' I appreciate that this neighborhood is *real*." An affirmative nod. "Real makes it better, oddballs included."

Renee waited for Anthony to keep going, just like he always did.

"I felt far worse in our first apartment. All these trees

practically swallowing the neighborhood," he nodded at the window, indicating sprawling branches of drooping leaves and flowers and not the still-bickering Ezekiel and Wendall, "make me feel more at home. This was the right move for us."

"Yeah," she nodded with a laugh, "a man selling junk out of his front yard is clearly more desirable than a coffee shop on the corner where I can order a cappuccino without having to make it myself."

"But you love the French press."

"I also love being served and having a barista—"

"I'll serve you," Anthony smiled.

"I know you will."

"Just watch, another few months, and everyone will be wanting their own junkman. People will pull right up to the lawn, then they'll roll down their window and order all of their junk in person."

"Will they also be wanting their own Miss Adelaides?" Renee nodded at the window.

Anthony followed her gaze to an old woman carrying a bag full of groceries from The Canopy, her back straighter than a stick in the dirt, an old-fashioned hat drooping low on both sides of her head.

"Of course," he lied.

Miss Adelaide was approximately thirty-four thousand years old. She had lived on their street longer than anyone and might as well have worn that truth on a T-shirt, seeing as how often she felt inclined to announce it.

The couple watched as Miss Adelaide approached the still-arguing Pattersons and shook her walking stick at them, clearly shaming the father and son for fighting in the street again. Both men hung their heads, Ezekiel walking off toward the bus stop and Wendall scuttling back into the house.

"You know what would be nice?" Renee asked.

"Another season of *The Wire*."

She shook her head. "If you could for once in your life acknowledge something for the way it is instead of the bright side of how you want it to be. I'm fine with the junk man and with Miss Adelaide and with all the broken pavement. I'm even fine with the Marshalls—"

"The Marshalls aren't that bad."

"See!" Renee laughed. "I can't even finish my thought about the way things actually are without you immediately wanting to make them better. I'm fine with the bootleg, so long as you're not trying to convince me that it's the real thing."

"I'm not trying to convince you it's the real thing." Anthony shook his head. "I just don't believe it's all one or the other. Sure, our pavement is cracked and patched, but look around. The homes all have porches and swings … don't you think there's something sweet about that?"

He expected her to reply with something like, *You mean all the homes that aren't boarded up?* But instead she said, "Yes, Anthony. There is something sweet about that. Especially our swing."

Anthony had never regretted the four hours it had taken him to put up the porch swing. He didn't have the right hardware, and it took two trips to the store to get what he needed, but when the job was done, Renee had plunked down on it and declared she loved it enough to sleep on. Her plan lasted only until the mosquitos came out.

Now she smiled, and it was like the sun got suddenly brighter outside and spilled extra light inside their kitchen. But then Renee changed the subject. Sort of.

"I suppose you want to tell me that your headaches are just tickles in your skull."

Anthony didn't reply.

"Have you gone to get checked out yet?"

He shooed her fussing away with a wave of his hand. "I already told you, it's just the stress."

"It is quite the strain ... always seeing the sunny side of everything."

"They say that moving is one of the most stressful things a person can do in their lives."

"Did 'they' take into account that we moved almost six months ago?"

Anthony had a lonely bite of scrambler left on his plate. He knew it would be cold before shoving that bite into his mouth, but a full mouth always beat an empty reply.

Renee said, "I know you miss NOLA, baby, but this is what you always do: pretend that things are better than they are so you don't have to acknowledge when you're sad."

"I'll be sad if I'm late for work." Anthony laughed, then turned in his chair and kissed her on the lips. "I'm fine."

"Yeah, you are." She kissed him back. "But you'll be a lot finer if you get those headaches checked out."

"Okay."

"I know that *okay*. That *okay* means I'll agree and then promptly forget and probably have an idea about becoming a standup comedian. Again."

"That's not fair."

"Agreed," Renee said.

"Ouch."

"Now hurry up and get to work."

Chapter Two

ANTHONY WASHED their dishes and silverware, then rinsed his skillet, trying not to think about how much he missed Grandmoh, and NOLA, and the old fish pond that he hadn't seen since he was seven, just like he kept trying not to think about all the ways Renee was right. Like usual. Or maybe always.

He did tend to look on the bright side of things. Optimism wasn't just in his DNA; looking on the bright side made the world a *much* better place. But maybe his declared outlook when it came to their living situation had been doing more harm than good.

"Love you!" Anthony called while grabbing his keys.

He made it six steps from his front door, still just a few away from his Jeep Wrangler, when Joy Jones hit the edge of his driveway, blurting all three of his names.

"Anthony Ray Joyner!"

He smiled, holding his sigh inside. "Good morning Mrs. Jones."

"You need to come with me." She spun back around a second after making eye contact, waving Anthony back toward her house. "I have three jars that need opening, and you're just the young man to make that happen for me."

"Of course, Mrs. Jones." He followed her, glancing at his watch, imagining his clenched sphincter of a boss, Scott Hodson, and what the jerk might say if his subordinate failed to be sitting and ready for work at his desk at least a minute before he was paid to be there.

Early is on time, and on time is late, Joyner.

He had to make this fast. Joy Jones acted like the queen of everything and handed tasks to her neighbors like old ladies were supposedly always offering butterscotch candy to kids. Time was like heat when it came to his most demanding neighbor; Anthony could palm a mug of piping hot coffee for a moment or two, but even a beat too long would burn him for sure.

Joy Jones had a trio of jars, as promised, lined in a neat little row. She didn't even need to point; he was already on them, popping the lids in quick succession and leaving them in an equally neat but now finished row.

Of course, Joy Jones waited to start on her first of likely many topics after Anthony was finished and ready to get the hell out of there.

"You know, Darius isn't quite the jar opener he used to be," she complained.

"Just think about all the jars he stocks but never needs to open." Anthony had no idea what else to say.

"That's exactly what I'm talking about!" She jabbed her finger at the ceiling in triumph. He had no idea why. "It's that place. It's making him old."

"The Canopy?"

"It's time he let go of the store and retired."

Anthony loved shopping at The Canopy. And not just because the bodega was on the nearest corner and, therefore, his and Renee's first choice by default. The store was owned and operated by Darius Jones, the wheelchair-bound patriarch of their cul-de-sac. The proprietor was kind, but he brooked zero shit. Anthony didn't know Darius well, but something about the old man reminded him of his grandmother.

"Is Darius really thinking about retiring?"

"Ha!" She snorted. "Darius is having none of that."

Anthony felt himself at the odd intersection of needing to flee and a strong desire to defend Darius. "Maybe he loves having a purpose."

"Stocking jars he can't even open?" Joy Jones laughed.

"He gets to talk to people all day. That keeps him—"

"He could talk all he wants on a cruise to Belize."

"Has Darius been talking about—"

"He could sell out and be done with it." She shook her head. "Darius doesn't even know what he wants."

"You'd know better than me." Anthony smiled, then looked down at his watch — Darius was now on his own. "I'm really glad that I could help you with those jars, but I'm running late for work."

"Oh, you just give them one of your smiles, and they'll be apologizing to you," said Joy Jones, as if she was offering a reasonable solution.

"I'll give it a try." He gave her another smile, then nodded on his way out.

"Will Renee be home later?" she called out from behind him, likely assigning to-dos in her head.

"I'm pretty sure she has a thing," Anthony replied, having mercifully reached her front door. "Good luck with the cruise!"

And then he was on the porch, trotting to his Jeep, now officially running late.

He sat inside and turned the engine, looking both ways before backing out of his driveway.

A necessary mistake, but now Anthony was back to thinking about some of those things he'd been trying to forget. All those truths about his new neighborhood that he didn't really want to confront.

He did like that the neighborhood was lively. Activity on Edgewood Street started early and ran late, sometimes from the same place, like the matching set of girls slipping out of what he and Renee had been calling BroHouse for the last half-year they'd lived there. The girls each carried their high heels in one hand while practically tiptoeing — opposite of the parade route they had seemed to be following into the BroHouse last night.

Miss Adelaide was marching up to the lawn, meeting the girls on the grass with a shaking fist, issuing scathing reprimands that Anthony could not hear yet easily imagined after having witnessed this scene so many times before.

You hussies should be ashamed! You're drenching your mamas in disgrace! Even the Good Lord won't want you after the way you've gone and soiled yourselves!

Anthony couldn't help but give the girls a friendly wave as he drove by them, running away from Adelaide, past the boarded houses — two in a row, plus a third across the street, all three foreclosed by the bank.

He drove past Wendall Patterson, now carrying his sign on a march toward The Canopy, today's message alerting the world in crimson words that sinners burned *HOTT*.

He didn't see Ezekiel, but the Junkman over on the corner was loudly shilling his wares. Anthony gave him a wave but avoided eye contact as he passed, not wanting to refuse the purchase of a broken toaster yet again.

Renee was right. He needed to stop pretending this was

Disney World and start being cool with the truth that it was a parking lot carnival, carnies included.

He slowed while approaching the corner bodega. Darius was out front, directing an anxious-looking employee doing his best to arrange a triangle sign in front of the shop to his boss's satisfaction.

Anthony raised his hand to give old Mr. Jones a wave, but then it fell involuntarily back to the steering wheel at the sight of three beefy men leaning against the building, one of them looking like he owned the place while the other two seemed like they might burn it to cinders. A fourth beefcake, even bigger and meaner looking, sauntered over with a short stack of plastic chairs as a fifth dragged a table toward their buddies.

187 Boys, the neighborhood gang, setting up shop for the day.

The last thing Anthony wanted was to shine any unnecessary light on himself or Renee. Everyone knew that the gangbangers spent most of their day smoking weed, drinking, and playing cards in front of The Canopy. They had been a neighborhood fixture almost as long as the bodega itself. Most of his neighbors seemed comfortable with the assembly of men who looked suspiciously like killers. Still, the sight occasionally made him break out into an unreasonable sweat.

Not that he ever showed himself in front of Renee. If she had been sitting shotgun right now, he would have acted like he was driving past a carousel. Sure, a neighborhood Starbucks wouldn't tolerate the incessant loitering, but when it came right down to it, he wouldn't have wanted to trade the comfort of a cappuccino to go for the authenticity that made his neighborhood a genuine place, and one that felt like an echo of Grandmoh's in NOLA.

So as he flipped on his blinker to turn the corner out of

his cul-de-sac, Anthony raised a hand and offered a friendly wave to his neighbors.

One of the gang members — who suddenly didn't seem mean at all while sitting in his plastic chair and tossing a deck of cards onto the table — nodded his way.

Anthony exhaled, surprised to find himself smiling, one step closer to being a great neighbor here in what was so obviously a very real neighborhood.

Chapter Three

BY THE TIME Anthony arrived at work, his headache had drifted from a mild annoyance into the boiling threat of an all-out assault. Knowing that his mug of Kenyan wouldn't be enough to cut it, he made a beeline for the coffee station, earning himself a dirty look (though mercifully no words) from Scott Hodson.

Anthony got halfway to his desk, with that first sip already leaving acid in his stomach while doing nothing to aid his headache when his best work buddy came up beside him.

"Smooth move missing drinks last night." Kevin clapped him on the shoulder.

"Oh, yeah?" Anthony turned to look at Kevin, already knowing some approximation of the answer before asking his question. "Why's that?"

Kevin shook his head in mock disgust. "Our fearless leader showed up and stole the stage for a rendition of 'Big Girls Don't Cry' that was only about three off-notes better than that time Hodson thought he nailed Meatloaf's 'I'll Do Anything For Love.'"

"Still better than the time he tried 'Lose Yourself.'" Anthony cringed at the memory. "Some songs just aren't meant for karaoke."

"Right," nodded Kevin. "Knowing all the words when you're in the car doesn't prevent you from sounding like an idiot while trying to spit them all out in between inebriated breaths. Those songs *never* work."

"Third Eye Blind's 'Semi-Charmed Life.'" Anthony cringed again. "That one always makes me think that white folks are delusional."

"Same for the Barenaked Ladies' 'One Week.'" Kevin nodded. "We all had to keep cheering him on, despite it being one of his worst performances — slightly better than Meatloaf, but still an award winner compared to—"

"'You Oughta Know'? Because I heard Alanis herself demanded an apology."

"My cousin already owes Alanis an apology for an unfortunate stab at 'One Hand in My Pocket' at last year's Diwali." Kevin laughed as they each claimed seats at adjacent desks. "I'm pretty sure that Hodson is about to assign us the Mow Me Down account."

Anthony turned to look at him. "The lawn care company run by his corny college roommate?"

"That's the one," agreed Kevin with a nod.

"Then why don't you look like you want to drive a truck through Hodson's living room?"

Kevin offered his buddy a shrug. "Because I'm bound and determined to do the bare minimum, and I encourage you to do no less than the same."

Anthony raised his eyebrows. "Is cheering the boss on at karaoke really the bare minimum?"

"Pay attention, Joyner. Cheering for Scott Hodson while he brutally murders some of Billboard's biggest chart-toppers is what *allows me* to get away with the bare minimum."

"And what makes you think we can get away with the 'bare minimum' with the Mow Me Down account?"

"Because Mow Me Down won't know the difference. Besides, doing less than our best is our sworn duty. Scott Hodson is a certified idiot. That dude does *not* deserve his job or his salary. Why should we do anything to make that loser look better than he is?"

"Maybe because it's our job, and I need my direct deposit to pay for things like food."

"Neither of us are in any danger of losing our jobs. Look around." Kevin led by example. "Does anyone look happy to be here?"

"I don't see how the average copywriter's level of joy has anything to do with our job security."

"We're good at what we do, and that means they need us more than we need them."

"Only if we actually do the thing that we're good at," Anthony argued.

"You do you," Kevin said, turning to his screen. "I'm starting on my faux copy first."

Anthony laughed, then let his buddy get to "work."

Kevin always wrote a page or so of joke copy before starting on the real words. Anthony argued that this was a total waste of time whenever his coworker tried cajoling him into joining the party. Anthony wanted to clear his plate faster, but Kevin insisted that ridiculing his assignments before doing them was the best way to battle his resentment and thus the only way he could ever go home on time with all his assignments complete.

They both loved writing and loathed their jobs as copywriters at ContentHive, seeing their time there as the corporate prison sentence it was. But they each had different ways of serving their time. Kevin was always trying to subvert his responsibilities while keeping that subversion relatively invisible. Anthony preferred fulfilling his commitments as resentments brewed and kept pretending to mind all the unfair assignments and needling from Scott Hodson only a fraction as much as he actually did.

Neither Kevin nor Anthony knew each other before starting at ContentHive just a few weeks apart, but it took just minutes for them to become buddies after Hodson assigned them both to a campaign for a toilet paper company — the absurdly named Ethical Wipe — then shot down every one of their many hilarious (and wildly inappropriate) campaign ideas. Hodson wasn't in the least bit interested in seeing if Disney would license Winnie the Pooh or in any way willing to acknowledge that Kevin and Anthony, working together for the first time, were really "on a roll."

They were copywriters paid to get other people's ideas onto the page, never to manufacture or refine those concepts themselves. That reality would have been easier to take if their assignments were good or their work appreciated. But most times, Scott Hodson seemed about as tone-deaf with creative copy as he was with karaoke, leaving Anthony to wonder how in the hell his boss had ever landed the job.

Maybe Kevin had a point about the faux copy. Anthony had been staring at a blinking cursor for a quarter-hour before their boss moseyed up to his desk, looking approximately ten percent as cool as he surely pictured himself.

Hodson glanced at the empty screen and turned his gaze on Anthony. "Hard at work doing nothing, I see."

Of course, Kevin had already hidden his faux copy and

appeared to be furiously working. He was always so much better at burying the evidence than Anthony. He even had a phrase he typed on repeat while thinking, just so that Hodson could never accuse him of sitting on his hands. Once Kevin finally thought of what he wanted to write, he erased his "work" and started over. The magical phrase that kept his hands busy?

Scott Hodson is a lonely man who fondles himself to pictures of Grimace.

"Grimace?" Anthony had wondered out loud more than once. "Why Grimace?"

He had never managed to get a straight answer. The closest Kevin ever came to explaining his phrase was a story about how the original version of McDonald's blob of a mascot was a total marketing fail. The character — Evil Grimace — suffered from an obsession with milk-shakes. The purple blob wanted them all for himself, so instead of luring children into the hamburger shacks, he scared them all away.

"What the fuck, McDonald's?" Kevin had said in conclusion.

"Writing is thinking," Anthony explained, looking from his screen to Hodson. "I can't just vomit my thoughts onto the—"

"I'd argue that writing is rewriting, Joyner. Look at Kevin. He's always working."

"Revision is one of the greatest pleasures of my process," Kevin said seriously, saving his grin for after Hodson had turned his back on Anthony.

"Our processes are different," Anthony explained. "I need to think."

"Could you maybe try another process that gets that final set of articles for Accountice?"

Accountice: a credit union client that seemed to

register their complaints about the copy according to a spreadsheet.

"I'm working on it," Anthony said.

"Doesn't look that way."

"It'll be done today. I'm sorry it's not done already … I've been having these headaches."

"*A headache?*" Hodson scoffed. "That's what women say when they don't want to knock boots."

Knock boots? Was it 1990 again? Candyman called and wants his euphemism back.

Anthony was considering his reply when the boss delivered one of the more inappropriate complaints from his regular arsenal.

"Anthony, we really need to talk about your hair. Your dreads just aren't professional. Have you considered—"

"Locs," Anthony corrected him for what felt like the millionth time, irritated enough to cut his boss off. "And like I've told you, I'm a locs guy, and this is my signature look."

If it didn't feel like an axe had landed on the base of his skull, Anthony would have delivered an argument with more intensity.

"Well, a good haircut is like a good handshake," said Hodson, like a certified asshole, before walking away.

Kevin waited six seconds, then swiveled his chair back to Anthony. "I was thinking …"

"Did it hurt?"

"We should start a business selling T-shirts with clever ways to say *I quit.*"

Anthony raised his eyebrows. "Do you have any idea how hard it is to break into the T-shirt industry when—"

"Do you want to play my game or not? Here, I'll go. My first tee will say, *Smell ya later!* How about yours?"

Maybe playing would help his headache go away. He said, *"Born quitter."*

Kevin nodded. *"Sorry for your loss."*

Anthony: "It's *not me, it's you.*"

Kevin: "I'm *not coming in tomorrow, because fuck you.*"

Anthony: *"Lo dejo."* Then he explained. "That's *I quit* in Español."

Kevin: *"Later, bitches."*

Then Anthony laughed and delivered his final suggestion — *Don't dread on me* — before turning back to work. He even managed to get a paragraph in before his phone rattled on the desk with a message.

He picked it up and looked at the screen, surprised to see a text from an unknown number.

Your work lately has gone from subpar to unacceptable. We need to meet at Colony Square, in front of the Starbucks at 10:00 am to discuss ways that you can improve. Otherwise, we will need to cancel our account and insist that Mr. Hodson lets you go.

Mystified, Anthony keyed the number into the contact search. *Becky from Accountice.*

"What the hell?" Anthony muttered to himself, turning to commiserate with Kevin.

But his buddy was jumping up from his seat. "Sorry, man, I've gotta hit the can!"

And then Kevin was gone.

Chapter Four

ANTHONY PUSHED his Jeep harder than the Wrangler wanted to go on his way to Colony Square.

He got the text from Accountice with only a half-hour to slip out of the office unseen (no way he was asking Hodson for permission or informing the boss about the nature of his liaison) then haul ass downtown. Anthony arrived, wondering if he would need a quick stop in the bathroom to mop the sweat from his brow, only to discover that it wasn't Becky from Accountice waiting for him.

Anthony saw Michael, his favorite cousin, sitting with a smile at an outside table for two.

"That *highly unprofessional* text from 'Accountice' should have been my first clue." Anthony hugged his cousin before taking his seat. "Asshole."

It was frustrating that he'd bolted out of work and infuriating that Michael had surely benefited from Kevin's help (that dash to the bathroom should have been his second clue), but the overwhelming emotion was still delight at seeing his cousin. Anthony never knew when Michael might pop up, so it was always a welcome sight, regardless of convenience.

"That's not the worst I've been called," Michael agreed. His booming laugh reminded Anthony of his uncle Jamal. "What have you been up to, Cuzzo?"

"Boring stuff, man. I'm sure your stories beat mine, so why not start there?"

It didn't matter what had happened in his life since the last time they saw each other. Anthony could have written a book, had a movie made based on that bestseller, then won the Oscar for best adapted screenplay — Michael would have probably had an entire awards show devoted to him.

Both cousins shared the same fun-loving attitude, but Michael had none of Anthony's sense of responsibility.

No one ever knew what Michael might do next. He had spent an entire year on a fishing boat before blowing all the cash he earned starting a bachelor party business in Vegas. The question now was, *how long would his cousin be staying?* Michael might be blowing through town or planning to visit for the next several months. Hilariously, or perhaps horrifyingly, Michael himself might not know which one it was.

But ten minutes into their conversation and his cousin's intentions became clear. "You mind if I crash with you for a spell?"

"What's a 'spell'?"

"Could be an incantation that makes someone love you even when they don't." Michael shrugged. "Or it might mean a week or two."

Anthony laughed. "Sure thing. But since your ass got me here from work, I still have to get back. Like *now*. So—"

"You think I can't find my way to your place? I already

—" Michael stopped and glanced across the street. "Why was that crazy old man looking at you like that just now?"

Anthony followed his gaze, then laughed. "Oh. That's Wendall. We know each other."

"You're shitting me, right?" Michael clearly didn't believe him. "There is no world where you're *friends* with that guy."

"I didn't say we were friends. I said I know him." He looked over at Wendall, who had already changed his sign for the second time that morning. It now read: *Whoever sows sparingly will also reap sparingly, and whoever sows generously will also reap generously. 2 Corinthians 9:6.*

"How do you know this doomsayer?" Michael asked, still in abject disbelief.

"He's my neighbor."

"You moved under a bridge?"

"A cul-de-sac. You wanna see it? You can go home and wait for me." Anthony nodded at the old man, now wildly shaking his fist at a cluster of women, bellowing damnation as they passed. "And you can take Wendall with you."

"Sure …"

Michael steeped deeper into his disbelief even after Anthony waved Wendall over to their table, all the way until the old nutter finally called him by name. Then he couldn't stop laughing. He told Anthony to "get on back to work," and that he "had it from here."

That's what Anthony loved most about Michael, he was always game for whatever was happening, even when it was bringing a crazy old man home.

The rest of Anthony's workday was miserable. Kevin had covered for his absence, which was the least he could do after helping facilitate Michael's prank. Then Anthony had to tolerate more than an hour of torment as his coworker constantly wondered out loud, and with a bevy of hilarious insults, what kind of an idiot believed that a client would aggressively text him ... on his personal phone ... to meet at Colony Square?

Anthony was dying to end the workday and get home, even more than usual.

Fortunately, Renee and Michael were waiting when he arrived. By a quarter to six, Michael was on his fourth story and second beer. He'd already been going for hours. He must have used at least half of his time to think up new ways to rib his cousin. It had continued nonstop since Anthony walked through the door.

Michael took a long swallow of beer once he finished laughing, then started in again. "Bitch, you never got away with shit because you didn't ever know when to stop. Your stories were *always* too damn elaborate. You might as well have been carrying a sign." Another laugh. "Like your crazy neighbor, Wendall."

"I got away with plenty compared to most people, just not compared to you. But it's hard to compete when your cousin is actually Loki."

"Uh-oh." Michael made a face and glanced at the window. "Bruh, you got some white folks on your porch."

"That's Riley and Rob," replied Renee without looking.

"They're cool, bruh, good folks," Anthony explained.

Renee answered the door before their favorite neighbors could knock. Riley and Rob came inside, Riley holding a clutch of daffodils from her garden and Rob with a bottle of Charles Shaw, the two-buck-chuck from Trader Joe's.

Though Riley and Rob often came bearing gifts, Anthony was always more interested in their anecdotes. The couple had lived on Edgewood for several years, making them keen observers and eager articulators who delivered their observations best as a couple.

"Riley and Rob, this is my cousin Michael. Please, don't believe a word he says. And I don't mean that as in, *My cousin might say embarrassing shit about me that I'd prefer you not hear.* I mean it more like, *Keep your social security numbers to yourselves.*"

Michael scoffed. "Problem with Anthony is that he sticks to the same stories, so he's not used to it when someone has something surprising to say. He's easily confused." A mischievous grin, then, "How many times has my cousin here told the story about how he and Renee met?"

Riley and Rob traded a look.

Rob said, "We don't know that story."

Anthony grinned at his cousin. "Bam ..."

"You tell *everyone* that story," Michael said. "Like, when you're in line at the cleaners, you'll just randomly start telling it to the person standing in front of you."

"When is the last time I went to the cleaners?"

"Anyone want to ask me when the last time he went to the cleaners?" Renee looked around the table. "Or why?"

"I'd like to know." Riley raised her hand.

"You seriously don't know that story?" Michael asked in disbelief.

"It's not that good a story." Anthony shook his head.

"Then why do you always tell it?"

It was delightful to see his cousin so perplexed.

"It's a *special* story," Anthony clarified. "It's the day I met my best friend and partner for life."

Renee said *awww* with her eyes.

Then Riley and Rob did the same thing out loud.

Michael rolled his.

"We want to feel special," Rob said.

"Yeah," Riley agreed. "Tell us the story."

"And why haven't we ever heard it before?"

"Because Renee has been trying to get me to *write* the story forever, and as soon as I tell it, she'll just get on me again."

"I'm not *on you*, Anthony." The *awww* was now gone from her voice.

"We met on November 1, 2003," he started.

"That's precise," Rob said.

"It's sweet," Riley added.

Michael rolled his eyes again.

Anthony continued. "The date is easy to remember. I had just left my job the day before. I'd been working at Georgia Tech and had quit to start a business as a ... I'm gonna need a drumroll ..."

Michael complied.

"... I was starting a business as a host for parties run by a local club."

"It didn't last long," Michael delighted in telling the room.

"I was out with one of my best friend's sister-in-law and her best friend. They were both in town visiting. We were at the club and all dancing out on the floor together. But I left to go to the restroom, where—"

"This is the funny part," Michael said. "Assuming there is one."

"—the attendant sprayed me with some cologne that smelled like seventh grade. I was joking about how much it reeked when I ran into Renee and her sorority sisters."

"First words I ever hear this man say: 'If I smell like monkey pee, it's the bathroom attendant's fault.'"

"Renee and her friends were all laughing at me, but then she complimented my shoes. I said thanks, along with some other stuff that kept her laughing. I found myself asking for her number right after realizing that I could never live without it. But my phone died, so I ended up giving her my number and asking her to call me."

"Pro move," nodded Rob in approval.

"*Matrix Reloaded* had just come out, so I asked her to go with me when she called."

"That movie can still kiss my ass."

"She fell asleep," Anthony explained.

"Tell them about the next date," Michael prompted.

"No." Anthony shook his head.

"What was the next date?" asked their neighbors in harmony.

Anthony sighed, knowing there was no escape. "It was a fashion show."

"*A fashion show?*" Riley and Rob traded a glance.

"What *kind* of fashion show?" Michael inquired, even though he knew.

Anthony looked down. "The kind I was in, okay?"

Renee laughed. Even after all this time, she still found the truth embarrassingly hilarious. Apparently, so did everyone else.

But Anthony didn't mind. By now, he expected it, especially if Michael was in the room. Whatever: that had still been the best day of his life. Because after the fashion show, he and Renee had eaten ice cream while listening to music and laughing more than he ever had. She was a lightning strike, and Anthony knew that another *her* would never hit him like that again. Their first date led right to the second, and that next date then led to everything else. Renee was a girly girl with one hell of a head on her shoulders. Organized and pragmatic, she was the grounding force he so desperately needed.

"When are you going to start *writing* these stories,

Anthony?" Renee's question was part standing joke and part long-term complaint.

"As soon as I get a new laptop."

"What happened to the old one?" Michael clearly expected a grand story, and Anthony was all too willing to oblige.

"Well, I was working out on a boat on the bayou …"

"Sitting on the porch." Renee provided the reality missing from Anthony's version.

"When out of nowhere, an alligator launched out of the water and tried to eat me."

"A bird startled him."

"Luckily, its jaws just missed my arm but went straight into the laptop."

"He dropped it, and the stupid thing hasn't worked since."

The couple shared a grin as the rest of the table laughed.

"Is that why I haven't seen a new blog post in a while?" Michael asked. "You too cheap to get a new one?"

"Things are tight since the move."

"But we're so happy you came to the neighborhood." Riley gave Renee a squeeze. "Even if you're too broke for a laptop."

Renee uncorked the wine and poured four glasses — Michael stuck to his beer.

"We lost another neighbor," Rob announced after his first sip of wine.

"Who?" asked Renee and Anthony in unison.

"The Carlsons," he told them.

Renee and Anthony shook their heads. The Carlsons were kind and considerate.

Riley said, "I heard that The Canopy is going to be a Starbucks."

Anthony shook his head. "I talked to Joy Jones just this morning. Darius doesn't want to sell."

But still, that one felt like a knife to the ribs. That was the thing Anthony genuinely loved about this neighborhood, the number one thing that made it all worth it. The fact that it was real. And now they might not even have that?

"So what, your cul-de-sac is gonna be at the corner of Gentrification and White?" Michael asked.

"The neighborhood will never stand for it." Riley shook her head. "It may get a Starbucks on the corner, and if enough of those old abandoned Craftsman houses keep on selling to hipsters, we might even get a Whole Foods over on Moreland Avenue. But we'll still have mean old Miss Adelaide."

"The Joneses will still live here, even if Darius sells," added Rob.

Michael nodded, wanting in on the game. "You guys have also got the doomsayer, and I heard he has a nutty son ..."

"Don't forget the Marshalls." Renee's nose seemed to wrinkle with the memory.

"They mean well ..." Riley tried.

"Do they?" Rob asked.

Michael looked excited. "Who else is in the neighborhood?"

"The bros in the BroHouse." Renee nodded out the window.

Anthony explained: "Three college dudes that live next door. They try super hard to be cool."

"But only so they can bed a parade of Instahoes." Renee rolled her eyes.

"I think one of them's gay," said Rob.

"But only so they can bed a parade of Instahoes *and guys*," Anthony repeated with a grin.

Michael nodded in approval. "Who else?"

Anthony shrugged. "We just moved in."

"You moved in six months ago," Michael argued. "That's two-thirds of a pregnancy. Empires have fallen in less time. You know your next-door neighbor, the man who runs the corner store, these two who are apparently always plying you with wine," he nodded at Riley and Rob, "plus the old lady who yells at everyone and the father-son duo where daddy wears a sandwich board. That sound about right?"

Anthony nodded.

Renee laughed. "Don't forget the junkman!"

Michael said, "Sounds like you don't really know the folks in your 'authentic neighborhood.'"

Anthony shrugged. "I'd love to know them better. But what am I supposed to do, go door to door asking all of my neighbors how they're doing?"

"What would you do if you were ten years old?" Michael asked.

Anthony considered the question while everyone eagerly awaited his answer. Then finally: "Offer to mow their lawns and then hire another kid to do it and keep two bucks a go as a finder's fee."

Michael shook his head, then looked at Riley and Rob with an apology in his eyes and an explanation on his lips. "Sometimes it takes longer for folks on his side of the family to work things out."

Riley laughed in concert with Rob.

Michael clarified. "What was your favorite thing in the world when you were—"

"Fish Fry!" The answer left Anthony like the world had been waiting to hear it. He smiled in surprise.

His cousin nodded, pleased with himself. "That's what this neighborhood needs: *a good old-fashioned Louisiana fish fry*."

Renee said, "We went to a fish fry at the church a few weeks ago."

"That wasn't a fish fry." Anthony shook his head.

"So you always say."

"He's right," Michael said. "Ain't no fish fry like a *Louisiana* fish fry."

"What's so different?" asked Rob.

"Different fish, different spices—"

"He means not *bland*," Michael interjected.

"—different music and a different *vibe*," Anthony finished.

He was suddenly animated. Like the flipping of a switch, he now felt very much alive. He started talking about Grandmoh's fish fries, and crawfish boils, now on his feet and practically jumping up and down.

"Next Friday!" Anthony exclaimed with both arms in the air. "It's Lent, so that's the *perfect* time for our little neighborhood to have a good old-fashioned Louisiana fish fry!"

Chapter Five

ANTHONY IMAGINED that he would be too excited to sleep. But just a few inhales and exhales after closing his eyes, he could already hear himself snoring. He slept like a log and woke up ready to put all of his untapped party planner potential to work.

But Joy Jones practically leaped out from the shrubs as Anthony made his way to the Jeep. He had to navigate the refusal of two separate tasks — one involving laundry and the other her garden — and three morsels of awkward conversation, including an especially uncomfortable bit about "the way things worked" with Darius. Anthony didn't ask any questions.

But he did stop to get a coffee at Hill of Beans because they were out of Kenya at home. And *out of Kenya* really meant *out of everything*, an oversight on Renee's, or (more likely) his, part. The line was longer than expected, and by the time he got to work, Anthony was a minute early and thus only on time.

"I got a great idea," said Kevin, instead of *good morning.*

"It couldn't have possibly been that smediumassshirt."

"What?" Kevin looked down at his shirt, which happened to be a bit more snug than he remembered when he last wore it.

"A stand that you can prop your head on so you can sleep at your desk without slumping over."

Anthony nodded. "We could add eye stickers, so your eyes still look open."

"*We,*" he grinned. "Does this mean you're in?"

"Of course, I'm not in — what kind of eyeshadow would we put on the stickers?"

"Depends on—"

"Good morning, gentleman," said Scott Hodson, cutting Kevin off. "Is it safe to assume that I'll have the finalized credit union articles from you both on my desk before lunchtime?"

"That is a *super* safe assumption, sir." Kevin nodded belligerently.

"Good. Because I'm assigning you Mow Me Down next."

"Me and Kevin have already been tossing around a few ideas—"

"And I'm sure they're all great. But we have our starting point. I already pitched them on a slogan myself."

"I can't wait to hear it." Kevin genuinely meant it, but not in the way Hodson would have wanted.

"*Greener is better.*" He stood back and crossed his arms as if awaiting confetti.

Anthony said what Kevin wouldn't. "That makes it sound like the business has to do with sustainability instead of lawn care."

"People know it's lawn care because of the name," Hodson defended his idiocy.

Anthony tried again. "Then they'll think it's sustainable lawn care."

"There's nothing greener than lawns," said Hodson, with a definite period at the end of his sentence.

And then he walked away.

"He puts the *ass* in grass," Anthony said the second Hodson was out of earshot.

"I was just gonna call him a grasshole."

"Much better." Anthony nodded.

His phone buzzed. He looked at the screen and saw a text from Renee: *I got a source for a fryer we can rent, but it'll be a couple hundred bucks. Gonna keep looking.*

Sounds fishy, he texted back.

Renee was in charge of finding the fryer, and he was in charge of getting the fish. So Anthony did a quick search before starting on his work.

But the window only stayed open for a beat, then the boss was behind him again, popping up like an Ass-in-the-Box, and not even to check on their work. He was there to share and bask in more of his brilliance.

"I've got another one," he promised. *"Green means go."*

Kev's expression really sold the lie that he was considering the value of Hodson's potential slogan. He let his face chew on the prospect for several seconds before twisting his expression into a knot of confusion and asking, "What does *green means go* have to do with lawn care?"

Hodson looked slapped as if he could not have possibly imagined having ever been asked such a question. "It means that you should go to Mow Me Down," he failed to explain.

Kevin and Anthony nodded, letting their eyes do the head-shaking for them.

"What were you looking at?" Kevin asked once Hodson was gone. "Was that fish porn I saw?"

"What's wrong with you?" Anthony shook his head. "Our cul-de-sac is having a fish fry next Friday, and I was looking for the best place in Atlanta to buy the freshest fish."

"I dare you to say that five times fast. And also, no need to search. I already know where to get the freshest fish in Atlanta."

But Kevin didn't tell him where that place was, only that they could go on a field trip together on Thursday. Anthony wanted to work even less than usual. He was constantly opening and closing browsers while exploring the possibilities for his upcoming fry.

After Anthony finally finished suffering the indignity of yet another day at a barely tolerable job, he and Renee circled their cul-de-sac, going door to door, inviting their neighbors to the fish fry.

Anthony paused outside of Miss Adelaide's house, just three homes into their mission.

"I don't know if inviting her is such a good idea." He shook his head.

"You don't know anything about her," argued Renee.

"I know she's a mean old lady who will probably ruin everything by being … mean."

"That's a really well-developed argument and all, but I think it would be rude for us to have a fish fry and invite everyone on the street except for her. Besides, don't you think Miss Adelaide is more likely to crash the party with a lot of shouting and fist-shaking if she's *not* invited?"

"I guess," Anthony said, but of course, Renee was right.

"Just let me do all the talking."

"Don't you always?"

"I wish," Renee grunted, already on her way to the door.

Miss Adelaide had it open before she arrived. "What are you two doing out there?"

The old woman radiated warmth like the dark side of the moon.

But Renee was a bucket of sunshine. "We're having a fish fry next Friday," she flashed the old prune her sweetest smile, "and we were hoping you might like to come."

Miss Adelaide raked her eyes up each one of them twice, then said, "I'll go to your fish fry, but y'all better do it up right."

"You don't have to worry, Miss Adelaide. I come from a long line of Louisiana fish fryers." Anthony glanced at Renee to make sure she was cool with him breaking protocol. She smiled, and he finished. "You won't be disappointed."

"They use all the wrong spices in Louisiana." Miss Adelaide sniffed as though something had rankled her nostrils. "This smells like a recipe for disaster."

Anthony felt something inside him crackle and pop. "You won't be disappointed," he repeated, this second time now with thrice the pride.

Miss Adelaide paused, assessing Anthony for a beat before nodding. "You can use my old fryer."

"Seriously?" Renee said.

"It's in the garage." She nodded. "I'll open it for you."

Then Miss Adelaide slammed the door.

The fryer was ancient and obviously hadn't been touched in years, but Anthony and Renee dragged the metal beast back to their house with a current of excitement rippling between them.

Renee ordered Michael to start scrubbing the fryer while she and Anthony concluded their invitational tour. Michael argued that his labor required some company, then he went off to recruit Rob. Together they sat in the side yard digging out years' worth of ancient oil from the fryer, congealed and rancid.

"That's nasty," opined Renee as they walked toward the Marshall's home.

Michael shrugged. "Sometimes delicious leaves a little nasty behind."

"You—" She stopped, both her words and her movement.

"What is it?" Anthony asked.

But then he saw. A tall, Black man tucking paperwork into a briefcase, nodding with a wide smile as he passed them, his glasses gleaming like he had a glovebox full of Windex.

"What do you think that's about?" Renee asked as she rang the doorbell.

"The Marshalls needed a socially conscious pic to post on social media."

"Is being Black socially conscious?"

"Maybe for the Marshalls." Anthony shrugged as the door swung open. "Hi, Ellen."

"Hey, guys! It's great to see you. Sandy's been wanting to talk to you ever since we got back from seeing *Unthinkable*." Ellen pet her ridiculous little dog, with no idea how insulting it was that she and her husband only wanted to discuss movies starring Black actors, in this case, Samuel L. Jackson.

Anthony wanted to get this invite over with yesterday. "We're having a fish fry next Friday. We'd love it if you guys could come." His tone had the relative warmth of a hammer hitting nails.

"Oh, I've never been to a *fish fry*." She said the words like *escargot* while nodding down at her rat dog. "Are fur babies allowed?"

"Everyone is welcome." Anthony smiled instead of

telling her exactly what he thought about her use of the words *fur baby*.

"Great!" Ellen exclaimed. "I would have no idea what to bring, but you know the three of us will be there and getting jiggy with it!"

"We should fry her," Renee said once they were back on the street.

They nabbed another three *yeses* before they were at the Pattersons' house with an invitation that apparently confused Wendall enough to get him talking in tongues before drifting into a series of threats centered around the book of Revelations. Ezekiel finally came to the door and steered his old man back inside with a firm promise to see the cul-de-sac's newest couple at the fish fry.

The BroHouse was most surprising. All three guys loved the idea and offered to help however they could.

"Don't worry about it," Renee said.

Then Jonah nudged his way to the front, between Carter and Josh. "We'll bake desserts!"

"Jonah sure seemed excited about the desserts," Anthony said on their way home.

"Maybe he's planning on making some special brownies. Or maybe it's his way of saying sorry for having a house that smells like a sex factory."

"It doesn't really smell like a sex factory," Anthony argued.

"I have a sensitive nose. On that note, you sure you got the fish all handled?"

"I see why you would ask now that Miss Adelaide solved your side of the bargain." Anthony laughed. "But yes, apparently Kevin knows 'the perfect place.'"

"Kevin does?" Renee raised an eyebrow. "Well then, Lord help us."

Chapter Six

THE WEEK FELT like a month as Anthony waited for Friday. Kevin could have made it easier by keeping his mind on work instead of using every opportunity to remind him how miserable their jobs were. "Wouldn't it be cool if we didn't work here?" Or "Do you ever wonder what this nine-to-five would be like if Hodson wasn't a tool worthy of an entire aisle at Home Depot?" And all while constantly teasing him about their pending trip to the fish market, his incessant mentions only making the grand event feel even further and further away.

By Thursday after work, Anthony might as well have been eight years old and on his way to Disney World. Michael secured all the containers, plasticware, grease, and sides from Sam and Son Wholesale while Anthony and Kevin finished the workday. Then the three of them met up at Atlantic Seafood in the Municipal Market to buy what Kevin had been declaring *the best fish in Atlanta* up, down, and all over the place ever since Anthony's first mention of the fry.

But, even as excited as he was, twenty minutes into their seafood-buying adventure, Anthony was staring into the eyes of a serious snag.

"You don't understand …" He shook his head, explaining the situation to Kevin since Michael was born to understand. "It's not a real fry unless we get crawfish for a boil alongside the haddock for our fry."

"Do you think if you keep saying the same thing several times in different ways, I'll finally hear you differently?" Kevin laughed, but there wasn't much mirth in the sound; he could see how down Anthony suddenly was. "You heard the fishmonger, 'cold weather this winter put the harvest under strain,' so that means—"

"That sounds like an insulting thing to call them," Michael opined, then repeated the word, tasting it like a spice on his tongue. "*Fishmonger.*"

"That's literally what they're called — a fishmonger is anyone who sells raw fish or seafood. Look around, dude." Then back to Kevin. "$3.29 a pound?"

"At three pounds per person, and sixty people, that's a couple hundred dollars," Michael repeated what had already been well-established.

"Did you hear that?" Anthony put a hand to his ear.

"What?" Michael took it as a serious question.

"I think they were paging Captain Obvious." Anthony pretended to listen even harder before shaking his head. "Must've been my imagination."

They wandered the market, lamenting the price of crawfish with no particular direction when Anthony spied a lonely canister of Tony Chachere's Original Creole Seasoning sitting like a lonely widow on the shelf.

"Holy shit!" Anthony dashed over and grabbed it. "I can't believe we got the last one!"

"It's not that hard to believe," said a voice behind him.

Anthony turned and saw one of the market's workers wiping a hand on his apron. "The owner brought a couple of those last time he came back from New Orleans. He didn't care for the stuff, so he decided to sell the spares. Someone bought the first canister about a month back. That one there is the second."

Anthony shook his head, holding the canister overhead like a trophy. "Imagine you were trying to make tacos but only had ketchup, and then someone finally offered you salsa."

"I'm glad you got it." The worker smiled, clearly not a convert to the creole way of thinking.

"You sure do love that shit," said Kevin as they walked away, and Anthony could already hear the rest of his joke. Kevin didn't disappoint. "You and Renee rub that all over each other or …?"

Anthony ignored him. "I've got an idea."

"Did it hurt?" Michael asked.

Anthony ignored that too. "I think we should get the cod."

Kevin shook his head. "I know you're better at words than numbers, dude, but the cod cost more than the haddock."

"But the crawfish was a bust," Anthony argued. "I say we get the cod and this canister of Chachere's Original and call it a win."

"I like it." Michael nodded approval, the Louisiana in his blood easing the argument for him, same as it had for his cousin. "Let's do this."

So they bought the cod and headed home, laughing and listening to Outkast, the trio arguing over which of their albums was best and wondering if Big Boi and André would ever get back together. Kevin argued for Idlewild as their greatest work, a record which Anthony appreciated more than he liked — the music was a little too stylistically all over the place to match the movie that went with it. Michael's favorite was ATLiens, but they'd had this argument before. Anthony remained convinced that his cousin only picked ATLiens to be a contrarian, seeing as Stankonia was clearly the better album. With "So Fresh, So Clean," "Ms. Jackson," "Gasoline Dreams," and "B.O.B. (Bombs Over Baghdad)," the winner was obvious.

The hook for "Ms. Jackson" was on fire for the second time as Anthony swung into the cul-de-sac, but they all stopped singing at the same exact second, prompted by the sight of Ezekiel and Jonah shouting each other down in the middle of the street.

Anthony lowered his window to hear the argument better.

"You can't just come up and take furniture off our porch!" Jonah yelled, sounding seriously angry.

"It was just sitting there!" Ezekiel bellowed back. "No one was using it, so why do you care?"

Jonah yelled something else. It had to be colorful, but Anthony was already pulling into his driveway. The Wrangler's rumbling engine muted the argument.

Michael sighed. "Maybe bringing everyone together is easier said than done."

Anthony put the Jeep in park and was about to make some lemonade from his cousin's lemons when the sound of Miss Adelaide shouting at the junk man for cluttering up their neighborhood screamed through the still open window.

"Fish fries bring everyone together," Anthony said with a note of defiance.

The guys unloaded their haul and brought the many

bags into a home that was receiving a furious scouring-down by the cleaning team of Renee and Riley.

"What are you doing?" Anthony asked.

"What does it look like?" replied Renee with mild agitation. "We're cleaning up for the big party you wanted to throw."

"But it's just going to get messed up again," Anthony argued. "And besides, no one's even going to go upstairs, so—"

"You want to throw a party in a pigsty—"

"It's not a pigsty!"

"—then you can throw it somewhere else," Renee kept going, her ire on fire and rising. "But if you want to throw your shindig in my home, then me and Riley are cleaning up."

Riley nodded along with Renee, saying nothing.

Renee looked over and surveyed their load. "That looks like a lot of fish."

"We got cod!" Anthony tried to make it sound like the boon that it was.

"*Cod?*" Renee repeated, already onto him. "And how much did that cost?"

Michael, Kevin, and Riley were all looking either down at the floor or out the window. Anthony's cousin recovered the fastest.

"Come on, guys," he said to Kevin and Riley, "let's get this fish put away."

"What are you so upset about?" Anthony asked the moment they were alone.

"How much did we spend on all that fish?"

"You're not mad about the fish. You were agitated before we even got home."

"I notice you're not answering my question."

"We spent more than we planned to, okay? But if we're

going to do this, then we need to make sure and do it right."

"And 'doing it right' means expensive fish and a dirty house?"

"The house wasn't dirty, and the fish will be worth it. What's your problem?"

"I'm sorry," Renee sighed, shaking her head. "I just feel like this is getting out of hand."

"It's not getting out of hand. We haven't even started."

"You know I like small, intimate gatherings."

"But the point of having a fish fry is so we can get to know our neighbors."

"Sure, but we could have invited them over one at a time for dinners instead of hosting this big bash that requires all kinds of prep and money and will ultimately only make it harder to know our neighbors anyway."

Anthony shook his head, determined. "This is how it's done, baby, I swear. This is how my family always did it. Atlanta and Louisiana are both in the south, but they aren't the same. In Louisiana, it's always, 'Y'all come in and eat.' If this is supposed to be about my settling into this neighborhood, then we should try it my way."

"We both live here, Anthony. We should both be involved in the decisions."

"I'm not trying to—"

"This is just like the time you tried to start that garden coop back in Louisiana. I told you to look into permits *before* you started telling everyone you ever knew about it. We spent months getting everyone paid back when the city levied all those fines. You get these ideas, and you go at them whole hog ... and it's like you just forget about me."

"I haven't forgotten about you ... I could never forget about you."

Renee's next phrase heralded the end of their argument — for now — and happened to be one of the things he hated hearing most in moments like this.

"Okay, Anthony."

And then Renee returned to her scrubbing.

Chapter Seven

ANTHONY FELT like he could finally breathe.

Friday was here, and the workweek was firmly behind him. A crisp but colorful evening blushed the horizon in shades of tangerine. The fish was prepped and ready, but Anthony and Kevin had to rush home to get the fryer started after effectively navigating yet another unwanted invite from Scott Hodson to join him for drinks to "ring in the weekend."

"I'd rather gargle piss," said Kevin as they walked into the house on Edgewood.

"Or kombucha," Anthony added.

"Is there a difference?" asked Kevin.

The house smelled as clean as it looked, and Renee met her man in the doorway with a surprise. "Look what I made." She pointed to a table packed with an impressive array of Jell-O shots in Mardi Gras colors. "Aren't they pretty?"

"Gorgeous."

"This is going to be one hell of a party," Renee said, letting him know she was all-in.

He pulled her into a hug. "Thank you so much." He hugged her harder. "For everything."

"The shots will be everyone's intro into the party. Riley and Rob are setting up a table outside on the sidewalk, and Jonah offered to man it. Everyone needs to take a shot when they come in."

"Even Miss Adelaide?" Anthony asked.

"Okay, maybe not *everyone*." She laughed. "Though I'm not sure it would be such a bad idea for Miss Adelaide to get down."

"LACY!" Anthony heard Michael exclaim.

He turned around, looking behind him past the open door to see his cousin's good friend Lacy — whom he had heard about but never met — walking up the drive, holding a handsome acoustic guitar in one hand and a bottle of wine in the other.

Keith Jones was two steps behind her. It was the first time Anthony had seen Darius and Joy's son since meeting him a couple of months ago. He grew up in the cul-de-sac with his parents but was now living in the city center. A bit aimless but determined to make something of himself. It was good to see him.

Keith was carrying a speaker the approximate size of a loveseat and an iPod that could have fit into a box of playing cards. "It's *loaded*," he promised with a satisfied smile as Anthony and Michael came out to greet him.

Five minutes later, the music was blasting with "Ms. Jackson" as an opener. To Anthony's delight and surprise, people were already showing up. Of course, Renee's Jell-O shots were a hit. Or, more specifically, it was jet fuel in their rocket of a party.

When Riley and Rob came up to get shots from Jonah, he'd asked them to man the table for a moment so he could hit the bathroom. Riley and Rob had handed the table off to Darius and Joy, and soon each person was waiting for the next to hand them their shot and welcome them to the party. The neighbors decided this was a nice way to play "pass the host-baton."

Twenty minutes after that first song, a line had formed, with a few of their neighbors making it longer by waiting for seconds.

There was talking and laughing, but best of all, there was plenty of chowing down.

Michael and Kevin teamed up to ruin the first batch of fish because they couldn't agree on the right way to do it before Anthony set them straight. The next batch was a breeze, seeing as he started using Grandmoh's tricks and jogging his cousin's memory. Michael took over frying while Kevin and Renee shuttled the fish over to the buffet table.

Once Michael took charge of the fish, Anthony moved on to working the sides, looking up to see that a few people were already dancing. The vibe at his fry was exactly what he'd been hoping for.

"What the hell did you put on this fish?" asked Rob from behind a mouthful of cod. "I've *never* tasted fish this good."

That question kept coming, but Anthony gave everyone the same answer. "One-half Tony Chachere's Original Creole Seasoning, and one-half pure love."

It was hard to get a full picture with his neighbors all milling about, but Anthony guessed that the fish fry boasted around forty guests. The music had everyone moving, and the fish apparently melting in their mouths, judging by all the smiles.

Anthony spotted something that brought him right back to his childhood fish fries: a cluster of neighbors playing cards at a folding table on his front lawn. The group included Joy and Darius Jones, Riley and Rob, and even Miss Adelaide and Ezekiel Patterson. He walked over, expecting to hear some friendly banter to accompany an amiable game of cards, but instead, he realized that there was a conversation in play. One that was already warm and getting hot fast.

"I'm telling you, that man is not to be trusted!" Miss Adelaide shook her fist.

She probably wouldn't have trusted Jesus, even if the Fisher King himself was offering fish for their fry, so that wasn't saying much, but Darius added, "I think we all need to be very aware."

"Aware of what?" Anthony asked as he sat. "Who are we talking about?"

"Eddison Fisher." Miss Adelaide might as well have spat the name.

"Who's that?"

"That Carlton-looking brother that's been sniffing around," Darius said.

Riley and Rob looked upset.

"What am I missing?" Anthony tried again. "Who is this Eddison Fisher guy? Other than some 'Carlton-looking brother'?"

"He's a developer," Riley said, making *developer* sound suspiciously like *murderer*. "He bought all of the foreclosed houses—"

"And now apparently, he's talking about developing the entire neighborhood," Rob finished.

"We didn't know because we rent, but ..." Riley seemed too upset to finish.

Anthony could understand how she felt. He and Renee had been living in her aunt's place, but only because she promised they could buy it from her. The situation had apparently changed.

The fish fry seemed too far away. Sounds and scents that had been filling his soul only moments ago were suddenly like memories he couldn't quite grip, muffled noises in the background of his thoughts, shoved behind a new and pressing concern.

Could they really lose their house and the neighborhood that went with it? He wanted to feel nothing but buoyant, yet an old emotion kept wanting to surface, that sense of sorrow and loss that had been inside him since that final fry at Grandmoh's when Anthony had lost something he loved.

He was only now getting to know his neighbors, as in *today*. They had chosen this neighborhood, not just because they had the opportunity thanks to Renee's aunt, but because the area wasn't gentrified and reminded him of Grandmoh and her little street. A cul-de-sac not unlike this one that had, in its small way, helped define who he was.

"What do you think?" Anthony asked Darius — as patriarch of the neighborhood and proprietor of The Canopy, he had the most perspective at that table. He also had the most to lose or gain.

But Darius just shrugged. "You can't stop progress."

And it was like a bat had been swung into the belly of their collective mood. Then the Marshalls arrived to sour things further.

Ellen pointed at the table. "Looks a little empty."

"Empty?" Rob and Riley repeated.

"She thought there might be chicken," Sandy explained.

"It's a fish fry …" Anthony didn't know what else to say.

Ellen made it worse: "And Sandy was really hoping to try some of those colored greens."

"*Collard* greens," Anthony corrected her, though, of course, she didn't hear him.

"Come on, guys!" Riley perked herself up. "This is a party! So let's—"

"PARTY!" Rob jumped up from the table, grabbed her by the hand, and boogied them both into the street.

Riley was right. This was a party. Regardless of what might happen in some future day after tomorrow, they should be focusing on happier things at the fish fry today.

Alcohol was flowing, neighbors were chatting, and thunderous echoes of laughter were almost louder than the music. There was plenty here to feel great about. Everything Anthony had wanted to accomplish with the fish fry was happening right there in front of him. Even Miss Adelaide was evidence of their accomplishments. He'd figured the old woman would be much too mean to enjoy herself, but despite how stiffly she sat in her lawn chair, there was no doubt about the light smile wrinkling the edges of her mouth. Surprising, seeing as he thought all the required muscles had atrophied a century ago.

Kevin and Michael were buddies again. Kevin had dragged him into a back-and-forth where each of them were pitching potential slogans for the fish fry, though so far, nothing had landed.

Keith moved the music from Flo Rida's "Right Round" — which semi-covered, or at least riffed on the 80's classic, "You Spin Me Round (Like a Record)" — back in time to the 70's. And with all that boogie blaring from his giant speaker, the dancing evolved beyond individual gyrations in front of patchy lawns to a soul train chugging down the street with pride. Even Darius and Joy took their pass, executing some impressive moves, despite the wheelchair. Ellen and Sandy remained oblivious in the periphery, doing a dance that looked a lot more like a dry-heave, but still, Anthony felt grateful that the neighborhood had showed up to enjoy the fry.

Swag surfing continued until the cul-de-sac was too exhausted to do much of anything beyond eating. Unfortunately, despite the abundance they'd started the fry with, the food was all gone.

But there were still plenty of Jell-O shots, thanks to Renee. The evening brightened, then dulled into a comfortable lull as the Joyners' front porch became a makeshift stage.

Partygoers pulled up lawn chairs to watch Lacey play guitar. Growing up in Louisiana, Anthony had seen musical marvels for nearly all of his life, but that in no way diluted the awe he felt while watching her fingers pirouette across the strings.

He sat on the far side of the porch, drifting slowly back and forth in what he thought of as Renee's swing, snuggled up to his wife as she brushed her knuckles against his skin, lost in the moment despite it feeling like they had maybe found another part of themselves.

"I think we just made Atlanta feel a little more like home," he whispered with a kiss.

But then the moment broke, much as Anthony hated that truth. He was suddenly thinking about Eddison Fisher again and all the things the developer might do to obliterate their dreams. He started pondering ugly possibilities, worried about losing opportunities that he was only now beginning to build.

Anthony looked up and caught Keith's gaze by accident. Judging by his understanding nod, the worry must have been clear on his face. He came up to Anthony after the impromptu concert and clapped a hand on his back.

"You can always go to the council meeting," he suggested.

"Oh yeah?"

"I went to a couple when that developer guy Fisher first started sniffing around, but whatever." Keith gave him a shrug. "I guess I had to let it go. Dad wants me to run The Canopy, but I'm happy with my job. It'd be different if I had kids, but right now, I'm not sure I'll ever come back. But if I were you, that's what I'd do."

"Thanks, man. That's great advice," Anthony said, wishing that Joy and Darius's son was around more.

He loved how the neighborhood came together for the party, but judging by Renee's expression, she loved that they stayed to help clean even more. Evidence of their grand event was erased faster than either of them would have expected, and soon everyone was either heading back to their home or already there.

Except for Ezekiel, who refused to leave. "You can't kick me out! This is my street too! You try and kick me out, and I'mma come back and steal all'a your belongings!"

But everyone either just booed the man or laughed at him.

Except for Josh, who said, "You better not even try it, dude."

"Ain't no fish fry like an Edgewood fish fry," Michael replied.

"True that," agreed a chorus of neighbors around him.

Chapter Eight

FIVE DAYS LATER, Anthony and Renee were spending Wednesday night at a municipal county meeting. So far, the event was only ever so slightly less boring than *Meet Joe Black*.

He leaned over to Renee and whispered, "*Is there a fast-forward on this thing?*"

"*SHHH …*" she whispered back.

Anthony managed to keep the comments to himself through the next several exchanges, despite what felt like a crippling battle with boredom. Talk of the possible development might sound like a bog of conversation to everyone else, same as all of the *blah-blah-blah* did to him.

He thought hearing about the value of a neighborhood and its citizens sure beat the endless back and forth of fighting for a freshly installed stop sign or that overheated discussion about how many pet waste eliminator stations to install at the new park that felt like it lasted for days longer than it should have. The only mildly interesting moment in the entire meeting so far arrived during a little hullabaloo about a parking deck currently being installed by Marta station, and only because a woman with a rather serious mullet stood up and screamed, "It'll ruin the neighborhood!" while furiously shaking her fist.

A man in a trucker cap that read *I'm not with stupid anymore,* sitting in the seat beside the empty one next to Anthony, leaned over and whispered, "Why are you here?"

"I'm trying to stop a new development in my neighborhood."

The man shook his head bitterly, then nodded like a sage. "They make you a decent offer on your property, then I suggest you sell it."

"Okay."

"Wait, and you'll get approximately nothing dollars, and you should'a done it differently cents."

Anthony wasn't sure that the man's argument would hold water, even if using actual numbers. "Or we could just *not sell.*"

"You won't get a choice if the county pulls that eminent domain crap. And guess what?" Another nod. "They *will* pull that crap."

"I'm guessing you're speaking from personal experience."

Renee pinched his leg; he was talking too loud.

But she couldn't stop Mr. Trucker Cap. "I was the lone holdout on my street. Now, I'm living on social security after losing my home and getting a nickel for it. So, like I said, take the offer."

"There hasn't been an offer," Anthony whispered. Then more to the point: "And besides, that can't happen to us because the development isn't for public use."

The man laughed — a tiny scoffing guffaw. "You think that'll stop 'em?" He had no intention of waiting for an answer. "No way. They make enough parks, and public use is automatically covered. Haven't you ever heard about Kelo vs. New London, Connecticut? Look it up on your fancy phone there — if that don't rile you up, then there must be something seriously wrong with you."

His phone was definitely not fancy. And while Mr. Trucker Cap sure had a lot of opinions, Anthony didn't get a moment to reflect on any of them because suddenly, the Edgewood Street Development project was up next. His attention was pulled up front toward a person approaching the podium that had to be Eddison Fisher.

Unfortunately for Anthony, the man seemed born for this.

The exchange started out with the same dialect of tedium that he'd been hearing all night, but Eddison wasn't just ready when it was his turn to respond; Anthony's apparent opponent was the picture of poise. And his honeysuckle voice somehow turned the words "live-work-play development with mixed-use zoning" into something musical.

"Go get 'em, tiger," said Renee, squeezing Anthony's leg again, this time in encouragement.

He introduced himself, stating his name before declaring his passion for being there.

His heart was pounding with too many words wanting to come out at once. Phrases he'd been spinning in a cycle inside his mind were now either lost or tumbling in chaos. Words that were usually fluent on the page struggled to come together to coherence in this setting.

"… Sure, our streets are cracked and broken, and yeah, we have a local gang that's claimed our corner … and a lot full of junk for sale …"

Was he rambling? Yes, almost for sure.

"I'm sorry, Mr. Joyner," said the man at the podium. "But I'm not sure I understand what you're saying."

He looked to the compatriots on his left and right, noted that they appeared equally baffled, then waited for Anthony to continue.

"Sorry, sir." He laughed to let everyone know it was only nerves and not a lack of clarity or intellect making his message sound slightly chaotic. "I'm here on behalf of my neighborhood to express some concerns about losing our community ..."

Judging by the still-expectant expressions up front, Eddison Fisher's knowing gaze, and the hollow feeling in his stomach, Anthony still had a lot of work to do.

"We just had a fish fry the other day," he continued. "And it was really amazing to witness the power of having a small community where everyone knows each other ..."

A twitter of laughter rippled through the crowd, heating him with a flush of embarrassment. The only people in this room who cared about the fish fry, or maybe even *could* care about the fish fry, had been enjoying their Jell-O shots and all the dancing that followed.

The county commissioner up front offered Anthony a patient smile. "While I appreciate your commitment to your community, I regret to inform you that the zoning is already in place ..."

"What does that mean?" But Anthony already knew.

"It means, Mr. Joyner, that it is well past time to fight the development. The question is now about how much area will be dedicated to park space and how much of it will be commercial."

The rest of the exchange might as well have been white noise for Anthony. Every phrase out of the man's mouth sounded like a variant of *Sorry Anthony, but you're shit out of luck today, tomorrow, and forever. I hope you like Starbucks.*

"That wasn't as bad as you—" Renee didn't even make it three full seconds into comforting her man ·before

Eddison Fisher interrupted them, hushing her with his approach the moment she saw him. "Be cool," she said instead.

"I'm always cool," Anthony argued.

Renee shook her head.

Eddison extended his hand.

Anthony shook first, then Renee, though she made how little she wanted to do it a lot less obvious. He wasn't usually the judgmental type, but Anthony hated everything about this smarmy mercenary in his Brooks Brothers suit, with creases sharp enough to cut himself on, reeking of German engineering and leather from shoes that could have easily funded their fry, with all the crawfish and cod his neighbors could have possibly eaten.

"I'm Eddison Fisher, as I'm sure you know," a bright white smile that looked like he should be on a billboard off the 285 selling toothpaste, "and you must be that nice couple I've heard so much about living in Ida Warren's place. It's so lovely to finally meet you."

"Is it?" Anthony asked.

Renee squeezed his hand. "Yes, that's us, Mr. Fisher. It's good to put a—"

"Ida is already selling her place to us," Anthony interrupted, "so we won't be selling to you."

Renee squeezed his hand harder and opened her mouth to respond.

But Eddison turned to her with straight shoulders and confident eyes — clearly knowing more about their situation than either of them realized.

"It would be a pity if Ida didn't get full value for her home. I'm sure you haven't quite considered this situation from every angle, but I know how much Golden Sunset costs and a niece who cares about her aunt as much as I'm sure you do would want her to be well looked after."

Renee had no words. She barely had an expression.

Anthony wanted to beat Eddison Fisher over the head with his oxfords, but instead, he made Renee proud and throttled his fury. Barring the snarl from his voice, he said, "You won't get everyone. We're a tight neighborhood, and *nobody* is interested in selling."

"Fortunately for progress, that's *never* true. I've been improving property values for a while now, Anthony, and I've found that people want to make their lives better once I show them an easy way they can do that." He nodded. "A lot more often than not."

"Good luck getting that first one," Anthony said.

"The Marshalls signed last Thursday." Another gleaming smile, followed by a shrug. "Worst-case scenario — I've had this happen a few times, and it's never an optimum solution for anyone — we can always build around you."

67

Chapter Nine

ANTHONY AND RENEE were quiet on the way home, letting the Jeep's speakers do the talking for them. André 3000 declared that roses smelled like boo-boo from his side of Outkast's double album. The rapper fashionista had a point: *things that looked good weren't always so good in reality*.

The song ended, and Anthony finally broke his silence. "The Marshalls suck."

But then he left it at that.

"You've been stewing in your seat for the last ten minutes now, and *that's* what you finally have to say?" Renee shook her head. "You could at least detail their suckage."

"You know why they suck ..." Anthony pouted for another few beats, then went ahead and explained it anyway. "They had no right to show up at the fish fry after already having sold their house and not told anyone!"

"Sorry, hon, but like it or not, the Marshalls had every right to—"

"Oh, you're best friends with the Marshalls now? You

planning on having a dinner where you all talk about how racism is a thing of the past?"

Renee didn't respond. His fault for being ridiculous.

"Sorry. I just …" He tightened his grip on the steering wheel.

"I get it." She reached over and rubbed a gentle hand on his shoulder to soothe him. "And I'm not saying you're wrong to be upset — I'm upset too. But I am saying that like it or not, it's *their* business what they choose to do with their home."

"Can it be *my* business if I choose to leave a flaming bag of dog crap on their front porch?" Anthony asked like it was a serious question.

"Do you really want to leaving a flaming bag of—"

"No," he interrupted, only half-meaning it. "I just …"

For the second time, Anthony failed to finish his thought. And just like before, a gentle hand began caressing his shoulder.

He let go of his death grip on the steering wheel to aggressively rub his forehead, realizing a moment too late that he'd made a terrible move.

"Another headache?"

Anthony didn't need to look at Renee. He could feel the worry-like makeup on her face. "It's fine."

"Is that your diagnosis or a doctor's?" Her tone was uncomfortably sober.

"It's fine," he repeated.

"How many times do I have to ask you to get your headaches looked at?" Renee asked, clearly trying to temper herself. When he still didn't respond, she let the silence fill the Jeep before adding, "If you don't get yourself checked out by a specialist, then I'm going to leave you."

Anthony rolled his eyes, still without looking over at her. "You're not going to leave me."

She met his gaze in the mirror, saying nothing yet still somehow managing to say it all.

"Maybe I wouldn't be having headaches if the Marshalls weren't so—"

"No. Uh-uh." She shook her head. "You don't get to do that. The headaches are your problem, and now you're making them my problem because you've got me all worried. That's not the Marshalls' fault. You're overreacting, and both of us know it."

Anthony mumbled something under his breath.

Renee said, "You just got used to this street and decided that you liked everyone, and now you're pissed because it's about to get yanked out from under you again."

Following a mildly uncomfortable silence that lingered a little too long, he finally sighed and said, "Nothing lasts forever, but home is where you make it."

Renee looked over in surprise.

Anthony shrugged. "Just something Grandmoh used to say."

"Your grandmother is a wise woman."

No reply as he turned onto their road, passing The Canopy where an assembly of dangerous-looking men were innocently playing cards. Unlike last time — or every other time before now — Anthony was unafraid to acknowledge them. He raised his hand and offered the group an undaunted wave. He shouldn't be frightened; these men were a vibrant part of the neighborhood he loved and longed to call home.

"*Honey* …" Renee started as he passed their house, and she realized that her man wanted to make a pitstop first. "This isn't the right time, Anthony … let's go home."

"When is the right time?" He killed the engine and turned to her.

Renee exhaled loudly enough to let Anthony know that she was almost groaning. She knew him well enough to understand that there would be no talking him out of this. He needed to vent, and right now, that meant that the Marshalls had to hear him.

"Can I please just remind you that they're still our neighbors for now and that we don't need to have our neighbors calling the police on—"

"I'll be nice." Then he got out of the car, wanting to pacify Renee but unsure how much he meant what he said.

Renee took his hand as they approached the front porch together.

Ellen opened the door after only one knock. No pooch in her hand, leaving plenty of room for a full glass of wine. Her eyes widened in delighted surprise.

"Anthony and Renee! My two favorite neighbors. To what do I owe this unexpected pleasure?" She shook her head before they could answer. "You know what, never mind. Where are my manners?" Ellen opened her door all the way and gestured for them to enter. "Please, come in."

Renee crossed the threshold, and Anthony followed, his nose wrinkling in suspicion. He felt tempted to march into the kitchen to confirm his theory, but not before addressing a much more pressing issue.

"So, you sold out," Anthony said without preamble.

"I'm not sure we 'sold out.'" Ellen laughed, sloshing her wine and sending the liquid dangerously close to the lip of her glass. "But Sandy and I did sell our house." She shrugged. "It was just too good an opportunity to pass up."

"But you didn't tell anyone about it."

Ellen made a face, her mouth turning down at the corners. "I'm sorry ... I didn't know I was supposed to."

She wasn't sorry at all.

Renee said, "There's just been a lot of talk about changes in the neighborhood, and we were—"

"Hoping that our neighbors would stick together and help keep this place from being just another gentrified area capitalizing on low property values to displace an impoverished citizenry?"

"*An impoverished citizenry?*" Ellen repeated with a laugh and a sip. "Isn't that a tad dramatic?"

Anthony didn't answer, already on his way to the kitchen.

He went right to the giant pot on the stove and lifted the lid, looking down at a sight that boiled his blood, same as the bubbling water cooking the crawfish.

"You made the crawfish boil sound so incredible the other day," Ellen chirped as she entered the kitchen. "I found a real Louisiana recipe online. I know!" Another sip. "You guys could stay for dinner! Sandy will be ..."

Anthony couldn't hear a word she was saying. Crawfish swirling in the water below had him seeing red. He was vaguely aware of Renee's even replies to Ellen's jawing on and on with her bullshit. He was pure fury, forced to remind himself that the Marshalls were proud members of the cult of ignorance, whether they knew it or not. He would be a better man to stifle his rage at their audacity, enjoying his party after selling out and then seasoning his injury with the insult of stolen traditions.

But Ellen didn't deserve to hear what he had to say because she was too clueless to truly understand. It wasn't worth his wasted breath. And besides, Anthony might want to dump that boiling water over her head if he finished his tirade and she complimented him on his articulation. *Again.*

So he shook his head and stormed out of the kitchen.

Anthony was still in the fog of his petty yet no less infuriating war to register what Renee was saying behind him, but the words *Sorry about* were clear, which only managed to rankle him further.

He walked home so Renee could drive if she wanted to. He could get the Jeep later if not. But he wasn't waiting around for her to finish apologizing to Ellen on his behalf.

Into the house and straight to the bathroom. He ripped open the medicine cabinet like the thing had insulted Grandmoh and grabbed a bottle of Advil to soothe his pounding head.

All Ellen's fault, Anthony thought as he swallowed them dry.

After a long sigh, he stared into the mirror, wishing that he'd been more composed but no less agitated by the Marshalls.

Anthony heard the front door slam and knew he couldn't cower in the bathroom. Renee would be in the mood for the kind of conversation where he was expected to prove he was listening.

He anticipated Renee, but Riley and Rob had joined her, and Michael was pulling off his weeding gloves and boots. None of them smiling.

Anthony looked at his friends. "Why do I feel like this is an intervention?"

"More like a war council," said Rob.

"Assuming you've chilled?" Renee raised her eyebrows at Anthony.

"Do chill and war council go together?" Anthony asked. "Because if so, then I am definitely chill."

A spectrum of emotions circled the table, with each of them handling things differently, but Anthony was pleased to see that their anxiety was shared. Riley and Rob were renters with zero control over the situation.

"You should have heard how cagey he was," Riley complained about their landlord. "He couldn't give me a straight answer for even one of my questions."

"He's kind of like that anyway," added Rob. "I mean, he's been promising to fix the kitchen sink for two years, but when he saw Riley had a makeshift solution with a wrench, he dodged the question whenever we raised it. But I swear this time he was worse."

Renee shook her head, looking at Anthony. "I'm not sure I should be pressuring Aunt Ida to sell to us. She just had a second surgery, and for the care level she needs, Golden Sunset really does cost a lot.

"Darius," said Anthony after another several minutes of shared complaints without direction. "He's the linchpin of this neighborhood, right?"

"He owns The Canopy, his house, and another home intended for Keith to use when he has a family," nodded Rob.

Riley said, "Plus, everyone listens to him."

Anthony finished his thought. "It would be awfully hard to build around his three properties."

Everyone nodded.

"So you think we should talk to Darius?" Renee asked.

"No." Anthony shook his head. "I think we should call a neighborhood meeting without Darius or any of the Joneses so we can figure out how we can convince them to stay."

"A *secret* meeting." Michael rubbed his hands together and grinned.

Chapter Ten

ANTHONY'S IDEA for a secret neighborhood meeting was a hit, and thus the details came together fast. The get-together was scheduled for the following night, meaning he simply needed to eke his way through yet another shitty day at work before he could finally start solving a tough problem he'd been wanting to get at ever since the fish fry.

Unfortunately, Anthony's day was even shittier than he was expecting.

Scott Hodson always made things harder than they had to be, but sometimes he did it in the most insulting possible way. Like today, talking (down) to Anthony about his dreads yet again. His "gentle ribbing" was obnoxious and frequent enough that Anthony seriously considered visiting HR about the issue. Telling Anthony it was "just hair," so he should be open to changing it, was *not* okay.

Worse, after a long day of writing copy that Anthony had no interest in but was forced to absorb nonetheless, he now knew more about lawn care than he ever wanted to and was already wishing he could find a way to delete the unwanted knowledge and make room for things that mattered more.

He didn't need to know that the average homeowner spent 5 to 8.5 days per year caring for their lawn, that the average size of said lawn was one-fifth of an acre, or that out of the 50 million acres, 21 million of them were front and back yards. Nor did Anthony care to think about the 70 million pounds of fertilizer or the 80 million pounds of pesticides applied to lawns each year.

None of it mattered. The one tidbit Anthony couldn't help but ruminate on while pulling into his driveway, twenty minutes late to his own secret meeting, was that a well-maintained lawn could increase the property value of a home by 15-20%. With all the dead lawns looking as sadly abandoned as they did in front of the cul-de-sac's foreclosed homes, he saw a fight on his hands. He was further infuriated knowing that Eddison Fisher would see the same thing as a "good deal."

Anthony only spied Michael after he threw the Wrangler into *Park*. His cousin was across the street, helping Wendall into his house. He must have found the crazy old man downtown unless he had started doing random laps through the neighborhood again.

He waved, but Michael didn't see him. So he got out of the Jeep and approached his front door, wondering which of Edgewood's residents he was about to see inside. He hoped for a full house, so the number of neighbors in his living room wasn't surprising.

It was still a shock to see who some of those neighbors were.

Riley and Rob were there, of course. So were the Bros: Jonah, Carter, and Josh. But sitting right beside Miss Adelaide — far from a sure bet herself — Anthony saw two of the very people the meeting was supposed to be a secret from: Joy Jones and her son, Keith, both sitting with folded hands and tentative smiles.

"Hey, everyone." Anthony gave the room a wave as the door opened behind him. He turned around to see Michael entering with Ezekiel. "It's good to see you all."

He couldn't help but glance at the mother and son who weren't supposed to be there.

"I know what you're thinking," said Joy Jones, seeing his face. "I was just visiting with Miss Adelaide when we looked out the window and noticed you all were having a party. Seemed like enough people that it might have been a neighborhood thing."

"I told them we were here to talk about saving the neighborhood," Renee explained.

Anthony turned to Joy. "I would have invited you sooner, but I know Darius has been wanting to sell and—"

"You don't have to explain." Joy Jones laughed with a shake of her head. "I'm all for saving the neighborhood, and you were right to leave Darius out of it."

"It's not about leaving him out. It's more that we're hoping to find a way that we can convince him to stay," Anthony said.

"Well, now Eddison Fisher is offering him even more money," she huffed. "So if you all want him to stay, you'll have to come up with something amazing."

While Anthony would never have tried to pit a married couple against each other, he did have to admit that Joy and Keith on his side could only be a good thing. He gave the group another nod and repeated his earlier greeting. "It's good to see you all."

The room was thick with ideas, bouncing potential strategies like balls in a game. Keith kept squirming in his seat, saying nothing but looking like he wanted to disappear. Anthony understood: several of the room's proposals circled a plan of action that had yet to be given voice, despite the possibility falling through the room like drizzle before rain.

Jonah finally said what at least half the room must have been thinking. "Can't you just take over The Canopy for your—"

He couldn't even get the word *father* out of his mouth before Keith voiced his objection and turned the assembly to murmurs and muttering. It didn't matter that Anthony and Renee had only been living on the cul-de-sac for six months. Everyone in the room knew about the blowup between Darius and Keith from a few years back. Darius had been grooming his son to take over the family business for years, but when it came time to grab the reins, Keith had no desire to do so.

Keith shook his head. "I already have a life."

"You have a house here," Riley tried.

"Right. And I don't live there." Keith sighed and looked around the room. "I care about this neighborhood, and sure, I'd love to come back and raise my kids someday—"

"My *grandkids*," added Joy.

"—but that time isn't now."

The room bubbled over in some more back and forth, with half of the assembly arguing for Keith to at least consider running The Canopy (as if he hadn't been ruminating on his omnipresent opportunity for years now) while the other half asserted that they should just leave him alone.

Joy Jones seemed to be working both sides of the argument.

Everyone kept talking over each other until Miss Adelaide cleared her throat. "What about the bakery?"

A round of curious glances circled through the room.

Nobody seemed to know what Miss Adelaide was referring to.

Except for Joy Jones, a smile spreading wide across her face.

"Yes!" She shifted in her seat to address the whole room. "Darius had some big plans about ten years ago. He was looking to add a bakery to The Canopy. And not just an oven and a counter, he was looking into a whole extension."

"Why didn't he do it?" Anthony asked.

A wrinkle of regret creased Joy's expression on her husband's behalf. "He kept getting turned down for the funds."

Anthony had his follow-up ready. "How much would adding the extension have cost?"

"Round about thirty grand at the time." Joy sighed, her *thirty grand* sounding an awful lot like *a hundred million dollars*. "But with inflation what it is, we'll probably need fifty grand to build it out now. Maybe more."

Anthony nodded, already thinking. And he wasn't the only one. The room was alive with chatter, several people now wondering out loud how they might be able to come up with fifty thousand dollars.

It was a tall order. The neighbors in attendance were all doing their best, but none were flush with money. Anthony and Renee needed every cent they had to buy her aunt's house. Even if everyone in his living room right now gave all they could afford to give, the collective effort *might* make five percent of their required total.

"I was thinking ..." The room turned its attention his way, then Anthony finished. "What about a fish fry?"

"What about it?" asked Renee, her expression suspicious.

At least that was something; everyone else appeared clueless.

Anthony explained. "When I was a kid, our church was *always* holding fish fries to help with their fundraising. Maybe—"

"That's an awesome idea, bro!" Jonah exclaimed as the other two bros eagerly nodded on either side of him.

The rest of their neighbors seemed to agree, with several chiming in, offering their verbal thumbs-up to the idea, or suggesting ways in which they might get the event going.

"That last fish fry was crazy fun," said Keith with a surprisingly wide smile.

But Renee seemed uncertain, and after chewing on her objection through the first few moments of discussion, she finally voiced her protest out loud.

"Don't you all think that maybe that fish fry was such a success because it was so intimate? And it was barely intimate at that. Even with just our neighbors, it was an awfully big party."

The room was quiet enough to hear a rattle of collective breath as the crowd considered its response.

Michael, sitting next to Renee on the couch, threw an arm around her. "Don't you worry. You've got the dream team here to do it up right."

The rest of the neighbors seemed to sigh in relief and switched back to excited chatter, discussing the many ways the straw of their neighborhood fry might be spun into gold.

"We could charge $10 a plate," Anthony suggested.

Keith shook his head. "At ten bucks a plate, we'd need five thousand people."

"So, we'll do more than one." Anthony shrugged. "And

think about all the other ways we could generate money from our fish fries."

"Fish *fries*," Renee repeated, looking even more uncomfortable.

"We could sell alcohol ... or get a sponsor. If we can get enough attention, then the money will follow." Anthony could feel Renee's resistance, but that didn't stop his excitement from growing. "It'll be a Louisiana-themed fish fry — and what's more Louisiana than Lent?"

Anthony almost wanted to bow after a chorus of cheering, especially considering the surprise of seeing Miss Adelaide's participation. He hated that Renee's concerns were getting ignored, if not shouted down outright, but he couldn't disregard the glaring realization that this might be the answer to their problems.

Except for Renee, residents in attendance seemed to agree that it would be worth giving the fish fry idea a go to see if they could raise enough money for The Canopy to add a bakery. They could convince Darius that he wanted it later.

"Keith and I will make sure Darius doesn't know the real reason for the fish fry," promised Joy. "And I'll make sure to get in the way of him selling in the meantime."

"I guess I'll start cleaning, then," Renee muttered under her breath.

"I'll go get a toothbrush for the grout." Anthony chimed in, his heart relaxing as he winked at Renee and her face found a smile.

This could work ... *maybe.*

Chapter Eleven

ANTHONY WOKE the next morning to an unexpected cacophony, beating an unpleasant rhythm through the house as an awkward compliment to the brutal thumping in his head.

The headaches weren't just getting worse, they were growing in frequency.

Anthony ignored it. He went to the bathroom, where he rooted around in the medicine cabinet for his Advil, then set out on a little safari through his house to figure out where the hell all the racket was coming from.

Renee's claim from the previous evening that she had to start cleaning immediately wasn't an idle threat. She sure was in no way attempting to quiet her efforts. Most of the noise seemed to be coming from the kitchen, though the clatter and banging came in a chorus. Anthony expected to find his wife in the kitchen, maybe going through the cupboards. But he found Riley instead.

She paused reorganizing the cookware (presumably because she was cleaning out the cabinets) as he entered.

She looked at him, said, "Morning, Anthony," then immediately returned to her work.

"Hey, Riley," he replied, already on his way into the living room.

Still no Renee, but by now, he was wondering if everyone in the neighborhood was there, unnecessarily scrubbing his house down.

"Hey, Joy." He waved. Then again. "Hey, Michael."

Anthony finally found his wife on all fours, scrubbing the baseboards like there might be gold bullion hiding behind the paint.

"What are you doing?"

Renee reeled around and blew a gust of irritation through her nostrils. "What does it look like I'm doing?" No time for an answer before, "I'm doing exactly what I said I'd be doing last night: cleaning up for your fish fry."

"*Our* fish fry," Anthony corrected.

Renee turned back to the baseboard and started scrubbing even harder.

"Why are you doing work that no one will notice?"

She reeled around again. "Women will notice, Anthony. There's a lot of work to do, so that's why we're pulling together and doing it as a group. We're going house to house and cleaning every home that will be open for the party."

"Are we expecting our guests to go looking through our cupboards? Because Riley's reorganizing them and—"

"Riley likes to have things in order. So praise Jesus if she wants to help me more than we need her to."

"You're clearly not excited about this fish fry ..." Anthony tried, desperately wanting to see her smile.

"You know how I feel about the fish fry. But if we're going to do it anyway, then I'm happy to pitch in. I—" She narrowed her eyes. "You have a headache again ... and

I'm guessing you still haven't made an appointment with—"

"I'm going to do it." Anthony flung up a hand in defense.

"But you haven't done it yet?"

"I just said I'm going to do it, so, no, of course, I haven't done it yet."

"Did you not believe me when I said that I'd leave if you didn't get it—"

"Of course, I believed you." But not really. "Things have just been a bit crazy."

"It's a good thing I love you." Her eyes were smirking, same as her lips. "I made the appointment for you. Check your calendar."

"Thank you for that." Anthony got down on his knees and gave her a kiss. "I'd offer to help, but I know how you like your space when you clean."

"Well then, doesn't that make it an easy thing to say?" But now, she was smiling. "And don't forget that promise to take a toothbrush to the grout."

"Haven't you ever heard of a metaphor?"

"Haven't you ever heard of a false promise?" Renee shot back with a laugh over her shoulder as she turned back to the already spotless baseboard.

Michael and Rob left to pick up some fryers and grills from one of Michael's 'sources.' Anthony figured it was best not to ask. They needed the equipment, and knowing too much would likely trigger his guilt.

While Michael and Rob secured their (probably) elicit equipment, Anthony took a little road trip of his own, riding with the Bros, headed out of town in their van to a place Jonah had found called Back to the Bayou. The Louisiana-themed shop would supposedly have everything they could possibly want. The place was an hour and a half away, and a brewing conflict hit its climax exactly forty-five minutes into the drive.

"Wait." Josh shook his head from the passenger seat, turning to Carter behind the wheel. "You're getting this, right?"

Jonah raised his hand beside Anthony and explained. "Our passenger is a Saints fan."

"So, in other words, a fan of the winning team." Anthony's victorious laughter was infuriating the Bros, but he kept on doing it anyway. "Drew Brees managed a whopping 308 yards in passes—"

"Christ, it's not like they destroyed us. It was a close game."

"Close doesn't mean shit." Anthony was having fun now, watching the Bros get worked up. "What matters, in the end, is the team with the trophy."

"That was a shit day," Jonah sighed. "We ended up in jail."

Anthony laughed. "Okay, there's got to be a story there."

Josh turned around. "Yeah, some asshole fan on *your side* was singing and cheering in the parking lot. So we started pelting him with what was left of our lunch—"

"Started a massive food fight, and the cops got called?"

"Dude."

"Umm ..." Anthony was shocked to realize that his neighbors and budding friends had been the face-painted college bros who had covered him in spam balls at the big game. He'd been lucky enough to slip off into the crowd when the cops showed up, but clearly, the bros hadn't been that fortunate. "That was me."

"YOU'RE THE FLEUR DE LIS GUY?" Josh was

now practically shouting while the other bros fell silent in disbelief.

"Face-paint, flag, and full costume," Anthony said. "Every game."

Carter wrenched the wheel to the right.

"The hell are you doing?" Anthony asked.

But Carter was already pulled over to the side of the road, and the bros were all laughing as he killed the engine.

Jonah leaned across Anthony and opened the van door.

"You shall not soil our vehicle with the taint of your foul language," said Josh.

"He said *taint*," snickered Jonah, shoving Anthony off of his seat.

"Whatever. You guys suck." He got the rest of the way out himself, but even standing outside the van, Anthony didn't think that the bros would actually leave him.

Staring at the quickly shrinking bumper, he told himself they'd be right back. When they didn't, he took out his phone to make an unfortunate call while muttering to himself.

"The Falcons can never keep a lead. And they suffered the worst upset in sports history when they went to the Super Bowl. The score 28-3 will never be forgotten."

It was a long hour before Kevin pulled up in his beat-to-hell Ford Focus with Ezekiel riding shotgun, but Anthony did his best not to hold it against the bros. It was a good-natured college-guy prank. The kind of thing he should be able to laugh at, even if he was a little too old for that bullshit now.

Kevin rolled down the window and leaned over Ezekiel. "Need a lift?"

Anthony smiled and jumped in. "I can't believe the bros kicked me out."

"I can't believe I managed to convince Hodson I was heading out to do lawn care research. You owe me. Time to start singing my praises."

Instead of telling Kevin how awesome he was, Anthony sank into his seat, relieved to be back on his way again. But Kevin was happy to fill the silence with ribbing and laughter over Anthony "getting his ass handed to him by the bros."

Ezekiel laughed almost as hard, which somehow felt twice as insulting.

The jokes finally died fifteen minutes into the drive. That quarter-hour was followed by Kevin subjecting Anthony to Will Smith's "Getting Jiggy With It" before he finally snapped the radio off and said, "So, who all from work is coming to the fish fry tomorrow?"

"Everyone cool."

"What does that mean?"

"Everyone cool," Kevin refused to clarify. "Which means no Scott Hodson. And even better, all the cool kids have promised to keep the fish fry a secret from him."

Ten minutes later, Anthony still wasn't sure who from the office he should expect and was reasonably certain that either he and Kevin had different definitions of "cool" or his buddy was intentionally being an asshole.

The last fifteen minutes were Kevin prompting Ezekiel into telling stories that Kevin was sure to reinvent later. Like the time when Ezekiel fought a bear. Or when Wendall found an old coin worth over a million dollars before some bum stole it from him.

Anthony was surprised to find himself bouncing in his seat by the time Kevin was parking in the supply emporium's lot.

Back to the Bayou looked like a Louisiana nirvana. And inside, the lagniappe wasn't disappointing. Kevin made fun of Anthony's giddiness while Ezekiel wandered the aisles. They browsed a long wall of spices, Anthony filling his arms with boxes of Tony Chachere's. Kevin went crazy with a basket full of Mardi Gras beads and enough fleur-de-lis flags to pledge allegiance to every beignet in the French Quarter twice.

Anthony kept laughing louder and harder. "The bros are really gonna hate that!"

Ezekiel came up to join them with one hand behind his back. "I asked Gloria over there where we could source some meat."

Anthony followed his clandestine nod to a round and jolly-looking older lady in a brightly colored vest. "And?"

"Alligator and snake." Ezekiel nodded like an expert. "I got an address. And this voodoo doll."

Ezekiel produced the doll from behind his back like a trophy. The thing was hideous and looked like it might have been made from a pinecone and a patch of old carpet.

Anthony had no idea if Ezekiel was serious, and the doll itself was scarier than any of the Saw movies, but he took the monstrosity from Ezekiel's eager hand and added it to his basket anyway.

Ezekiel's address led them to a battered shack, sagging on the roadside where an ancient man with a face like weathered luggage sat in a rocking chair, puffing on a pipe and looking as cliché as a postcard.

The meat man was happy to see them, greeting their arrival by leaping up from his seat and waving them in.

"Name's Caliste," he said by way of introduction, his smile crooked yet friendly. "Laissez les bon temp rouler with some meat?"

Anthony wanted to hug the man.

"You got snake?" Ezekiel sounded like he expected a *no*.

"I got it all," laughed Caliste, waving them toward his shack. "Come."

Caliste not only had the meat they were looking for, he had recently finished a fresh batch of boudin — a creole sausage made with rice, spices, and meats. Caliste was happy to send them on their way with some meat but even happier that they agreed to join him for a meal.

The food was delicious, and the music even better.

Anthony shook his head in pleasant wonder. "It's been forever since I've heard zydeco."

"Music for the soul," said Caliste.

"Sounds like home," replied Anthony, mostly to himself.

"That it does." Caliste gave him a nod. "I know a few great zydeco bands in the area if you're interested."

Anthony was still nodding; that pleasant wonder had yet to leave him. "I'm surprised how easy it's been to get everything we need for our fish fry. The right food, the right spices, and now the right music."

The crooked smile returned to Caliste's face, this time seasoned with wisdom. "There's a little bit of Louisiana everywhere if you just know how to look for it."

Chapter Twelve

ANTHONY HOPED for a pat on the head for his many fish fry-related accomplishments. Instead, their dinner was all business, with Renee wanting to cover the rest of the plan.

"Have you handled security yet?"

"No." Anthony smiled. "But I got us a band!"

"A band?" Renee looked approximately one-quarter as delighted as she should be.

"A zydeco band. Big Shorty and the Bayou Roundabouts."

"Where are we going to put this band? And how many of those Roundabouts are we paying for?"

"On the porch, of course."

Renee gave him a look, but she didn't press the question. "Did the bros find you?"

"Were they looking for me?"

"Jonah says they left you on the side of the road."

"Kevin picked me up. Then we went and got everything with Ezekiel."

"That part was missing from your earlier stories."

"I didn't want to get mad again. They—" Anthony stopped. "Did you—"

"I heard it," Renee replied with a nod, already out of her seat.

They stood at the window together, watching as Eddison Fisher scurried to his car, getting chased away from the Patterson place by what had to be the bros, though it was hard to be sure considering their costumes. Even if it was Jonah, Carter, and Josh, Anthony couldn't tell the three bros apart. One ran around in his underwear. That was *probably* Jonah. Carter might have been in a parka and a Darth Vader mask, which meant that Josh was wearing the wetsuit and wielding a hockey stick.

Eddison scrambled into his Mercedes and raced away.

The bros chased him for several houses before stopping to double over with laughter that Anthony and Renee could see but not hear from the window.

"You should talk to them," Renee said.

"I don't want to—"

But Renee was already on her way outside.

Anthony followed, grumbling under his breath.

One of the bros must have seen Renee right as she opened the door because, by the time Anthony stepped out behind her, all three of them were running toward the porch.

"Sorry, man," Jonah spoke first. He was indeed the bro in his underwear.

Carter shook his head. "Not cool of us."

Josh went last. "Even if Saints fans are only slightly better than Hitler, that's still no excuse."

"Dude," said Jonah and Carter together.

"We suck," amended Josh.

"It's fine," Anthony told them. "What was that all about?"

"Exactly what it looked like," Jonah sort of answered.

"Dumbass didn't get the memo that we don't want him anywhere around here," added Josh.

"Are we cool?" Carter asked.

Anthony hesitated only a moment before nodding. "We're cool."

Jonah stood there in his underwear, offering Anthony a smile and a shrug. "Anything we can do to be cooler? You know ... is there a way we can make up for being dickbags?"

Anthony rolled his eyes and invited the bros inside. "I still took care of getting all the supplies, but if you want to come inside, you can help us solve a much bigger problem."

"Mind if we change first?" Jonah asked with a laugh.

"I mind if you *don't* change." Anthony shook his head.

Fifteen minutes later, they had finished their now-cold dinner, and Anthony was enlisting the bros to help him deliver on his promise to Renee.

He led them all down the street, holding a plate of boudin on their way to The Canopy.

He stopped at the corner, swallowing hard to gather his courage, reminding himself that he was being ridiculous. So what if the three men loitering in front of the bodega were all members of the same gang? That didn't make Anthony their enemy. And they might welcome a chance to protect their neighborhood if given the chance.

"Hey, guys!" Anthony waved as he approached, wondering if the bros could feel his timidity. Or worse, if the men at the table knew he was scared.

"Hey," nodded the man with no visible tattoos.

"Hey," echoed the other two.

"You like Louisiana food?" Anthony presented his plate as the bros crowded around behind him.

The one wearing a superfluous coat said, "What's it taste like?"

"Delicious," Jonah declared, though he hadn't actually tried it.

"Delicious," Anthony repeated, extending the plate in offering. "This is called boudin. It's a creole sausage made with rice."

The men looked tentative, but the shortest among them was daring. He reached out and snatched one of the sausages, then shoved it into his mouth.

"My moms used to make something like this," he said while chewing.

The man with the tattoo went next, followed by the one in a superfluous coat.

"May I?" Shorty nodded at the plate.

Anthony handed it to him. "It's all yours."

All three grabbed for more sausage, No Tattoo, and Unnecessary Coat, now making *mmmm*s with their mouths.

"Awesome, right?" Carter said.

But none of the bros had tasted the boudin. Anthony had only brought them along to curb his fear. Yet, there was nothing to be scared of, and maybe he'd been a bit of a jerk for thinking otherwise.

"Thanks for the food," Shorty said, extending a hand. "Name's Manny. This is Troy and Xavier. Now, if you don't mind my asking, what's with all the free food?"

"Manny ain't implying we don't appreciate it or nothing. It's just not regular," said Xavier, the man without tattoos.

To Anthony's surprise, the bros were a rat-a-tat of replies. Jonah, Carter, then Josh.

"We're trying to save the neighborhood."

"With a fish fry."

"And we're going to need some security."

Anthony nodded. "What they said."

The men traded glances. Troy and Xavier both nodded at Manny, then Manny turned to Anthony. "There gonna be some more of this boudin?"

Anthony nodded again. "And all the fish you can eat."

"We'll be there," said Troy and Xavier together before Manny could get the words out of his mouth.

"That's great to hear!" Anthony said as Joy Jones came out of The Canopy, smiling at the sight of him.

"Mr. Joyner!" she exclaimed. "It's good to see you."

"And why is that?" Anthony expected a chore.

"I posted a bulletin at the church about the fry, and Keith promised to share it on Tweeter—"

"It's *Twitter,*" Jonah interjected.

"—so we should have an excellent turnout!"

Anthony nodded at his new friends. "Manny, Troy, and Xavier here are handling security."

Joy Jones smiled wide, and Anthony felt another wave of relief.

"I bet we'll get fifty to sixty people at this rate." He turned to offer the bros a high-five, but they were already on their way to slapping palms with the gang.

Chapter Thirteen

THE SECOND FISH fry was finally here.

Anthony could barely sleep, and according to the tossing and turning (and huffing and puffing) beside him in bed, the obsession with how things were going to go wasn't just preventing his rest; it seemed to be irritating his wife as well. But he kept his eyes closed, willing himself to sleep while picturing a happy horde of neighbors laughing and dancing at the fry.

The real-life setup looked exactly like he'd imagined. Grills and fryers were lined up along their sideyard. Reticent as Renee might have been, she was all in once the fish fry became a reality.

This time there were two tables full of shots instead of just the one, in all of the Jell-O in bright green and purple. The bros didn't complain, helping to hang a parade's worth of fleur-de-lis flags around the cul-de-sac in preparations. Keith Jones might not have wanted to live on Edgewood anymore, but that didn't stop him from showing up before most of his neighbors, this time with a full DJ setup and his buddy, DJ Donkey, the pair of them ready to play all through the day and well into the night.

Things started out great. Following the success of their first fish fry, the tradition of each guest waiting at the shot table to introduce themselves to the party with some alcoholic Jell-O had been formalized. Neighbors lined up, waiting for their shots while gelling with the person either in front or behind them.

But their little gathering kept getting bigger and bigger, until the fifty to sixty expected guests had ballooned into what Anthony guessed had to be a hundred heads or more — hard to tell with everyone going in and out of homes, both with and without plates piled high with heaps of food ... food that despite their best preparations appeared to be running out fast.

Anthony realized that they were perhaps out of their element as he saw Miss Adelaide shaking her head in disgust, walking back toward her home at the sight of yet another carload of people — strangers to him and surely to her — swinging into the cul-de-sac, then cruising around while looking for a place to park.

They might as well have been trying to find the Fountain of Youth.

"We have maybe an hour before we run out of food," Anthony whispered to Michael, hoping that Renee didn't see his covert exchange and wonder what he was up to.

"I'm already on it," Michael said, meaning he'd already spoken to the bros.

And like a good game of cul-de-sac telephone, they had spread the message to some of their neighbors, including Renee.

Now those fine folks were raiding their own kitchens for food that could be fried or grilled to keep the still-arriving guests from revolting. Anthony covered everything in Tony Chachere's, but his best efforts were never enough to meet the constantly growing demand.

"Why you charging for plates?" complained a loud girl with even louder hair — she didn't live on Edgewood, and Anthony had never seen her before. "You think you're too good for the hood now?"

She wasn't the first to snap at him that way, nor was Anthony the only neighbor to field that complaint. He tried to explain the situation, detailing the group effort to save their cul-de-sac from the ravages of gentrification, but either their explanations weren't translating, or they were falling on deaf ears.

Once the food had run out again — temporarily, Anthony hoped just like every time before — he took a break to use the restroom. But the loud girl with the louder hair was in his living room. She dropped her drink as he entered the front door, spilling a rum and Coke onto their floor.

The girl clearly didn't care.

But Renee was right next to her, and she absolutely did. "Would you mind cleaning that up?"

The request left her lips with more kindness than her eyes were implying.

The girl scoffed loudly, of course. "Relax. You don't own this party."

Anthony went over to Renee and took her gently by the arm, leading his wife away from the loud girl with the even louder hair before Renee became the loudest thing of all.

He looked her in the eyes and said, "Thank you for all of this. I really appreciate it."

"I know, Anthony."

"Would you mind going outside and telling DJ Donkey to change the music?"

"Change it to what?" she sounded suspicious.

"Something we can dance to."

Renee nodded, then left without another word.

Anthony approached the loud girl with the louder hair and told her that if she wouldn't mind going outside and starting the soul train line, he'd be happy to clean the spilled drink.

She replied with a roll of her eyes and a sashay out the door, then finally into the street, where she started dancing with gyrating motions that were somehow even louder than her hair.

Anthony turned from the window, then went to the kitchen for a towel. By the time he had finished cleaning up and was back outside, the girl had already inspired a soul train and had its engine chugging down the front lawn. It was big and rowdy and tons of fun. Despite the entire event teetering on the edge of chaos, laughter echoed everywhere, and a good time was clearly being had by all.

Except perhaps for Miss Adelaide, who barricaded herself back home and now had her shades all drawn.

After boogying down with his neighbors, Anthony went to look for Renee. He couldn't find her outside, so he went back inside the house.

But she wasn't in their house or in any of the next three homes he checked. After another quarter hour outside, Anthony returned to the start, reentering his own living room to find Renee cuddling on the couch with a dog who was adorable enough to go viral, sitting next to a woman he did not recognize.

Renee was wearing a radiant smile and seemed to be recovering from a healthy round of laughter. Anthony felt a bottomless relief, seeing her happy.

"Whose dog is that?" he asked, approaching the couch.

Renee looked up at him.

Then so did the woman. "The people who live here, of course."

Renee and Anthony looked at each other, then burst into laughter.

Anthony said, "*We* live here."

She abruptly let go of the dog.

It scampered off the couch and into the crowd, wagging its tail all the way and leaving Renee and Anthony in a fit of laughter.

Renee turned toward the window. "Sounds like the band is getting started."

Anthony had no idea if she was stating a fact or registering a complaint, considering the commotion outside. "I'll go and check."

Big Shorty and the Bayou Roundabouts were taking the stage, the lot of them barely squeezing onto the porch as a cadre of neighbors nestled into the corner, four of them trying to share a swing made for two.

The chain snapped, and the entire swing crashed to the porch in a furious clatter. Wood cleaved like half a glacier falling into the ocean, and four of his neighbors were tossed to the ground.

But there weren't any broken bones, and everyone was laughing, both the fallen and the partygoers. He wanted to think *No harm, no foul*, but Anthony couldn't stop picturing Renee and her likely response to the ruined swing.

The laughter died, and the music started. Big Shorty and the Bayou Roundabouts sounded even better than their demo. Anthony looked up and down the street at a fish fry that was vibrantly alive, though also chaotic.

Drinks flowed as the party kept getting livelier.

Troy and Jamal had to chase away a car full of guys who started arguing over a girl before their verbal scuffle turned into a physical brawl. They showed up uninvited, apparently — none of Anthony's neighbors admitted to knowing or even recognizing the guys — and were a problem almost immediately.

Looking to make a kick-ass entrance, Ezekiel conducted a running leap to launch himself through the window. An epic stunt, if he'd remembered to open it. Instead, he crashed through the glass, landing miraculously unscathed on the other side as broken shards rained all around him, somehow leaving the lucky daredevil untouched.

The Junkman was shilling wares on his front lawn, but for once, no one objected. Guests who didn't live on the cul-de-sac assumed it was part of the theme. He stayed consistently busy. Anthony looked over several times throughout the day, wondering if maybe Mr. Junkman was making more money on the fish fry than the neighborhood.

The party never quite spiraled out of control. Though Carter did bring things to a literal crashing halt. Anthony had no idea how much the kid had been drinking or how thoroughly drunk Carter was when he started screaming "KEVIN MCCALLISTER!" at the top of his lungs, apparently wanting to pull a Home Alone as he set up a luge on the staircase.

Of course, Anthony protested, but Carter was thoroughly smashed as he settled onto his sled atop the stairs, fashioned from a flattened cardboard box.

But instead of making it out the door, Carter landed at the foot of the stairs and cracked his head on the baseboard. Renee rushed inside too late, entering the house to investigate the deafening THUD instead of the commotion preceding it.

Someone called 911 a beat after Carter hit the wall,

and sirens were wailing before Renee finished mopping the still-dripping blood from his forehead.

She looked up at Anthony with panicked eyes and a haggard whisper. "You do know we're liable for this." It wasn't a question.

"It's Carter. You know he's not going to sue."

Renee narrowed her eyes at Anthony. Carter murmured something unintelligible. Even his vocal cords sounded bruised.

"I promise I'll line up insurance for the next one!" Anthony said.

"The next one!" Renee threw her hands into the air. "You've gotta be goddamned kidding me."

She shoved the blood-covered towel into Anthony's hands and stomped off, perhaps to greet the paramedics pulling up outside but more likely to vent her fury in isolation.

He didn't want to see her upset and did feel bad, but that emotion warred with the sound of joy all around him. Loud enthusiasm as a crowd of neighbors and strangers dispersed.

"Epic!"

"That was crazy."

"No fish fry is *ever* gonna beat that one!"

To that last one, Anthony disagreed.

Chapter Fourteen

ANTHONY HAD CONSUMED a moderate amount of alcohol at the second fry, but his head was splitting down the center like he'd swallowed a keg all by his lonesome. Or maybe like someone had hit him in the skull with an axe.

He rubbed his temples, consciously aware of the gesture, glad that Renee was already out of bed so—

He swallowed hard with the realization that Renee probably wasn't out running. She was likely looking around the house, either surveying the damage or already tending to it. He would be joining her in the cleanup immediately, assuming he knew what was good for him.

Anthony went to the bathroom and then downstairs. He hadn't smelled coffee upon waking, so he hadn't exactly expected to see a semi-full French press, but the empty counter was still an odd sight considering he couldn't remember the last time Renee had risen before him without making coffee.

Except, the counter wasn't really empty. It was filled with cups and dishes, plus several wads of mysterious packaging. He got the coffee started and then investigated the fallout.

He hadn't forgotten about Ezekiel's attempt to fly through the closed window, but the shattered glass was still jarring, cardboard covering the aperture to make the situation seem somehow worse instead of better.

The house was a mess, but as Anthony stepped out onto his porch, he saw that the rest of Edgewood was in a similar state. He donned a pair of thick boots from the closet by the door and walked outside toward the collection of neighbors cleaning the street, paranoid about stepping on broken glass despite his heavy heels.

He looked around. Still no Renee. But the mood was light despite the mess.

"DUDE," Josh said.

Anthony wanted to ask how Carter was doing — neither he nor Jonah were in sight — but Riley and Rob walked over with Michael, and Michael (to no one's surprise) was already talking.

"That sure wasn't Grandmoh's Fish Fry."

Riley said, "We narrowly avoided disaster."

Rob shrugged. "The operative word is *avoided*."

"Come on." Michael waved Anthony toward his home as though he was the one who owned the place. "Rob and I will help you clean up."

"We need better security," Rob said as the door swung shut behind them. "I'm glad we had the bodega dudes, but we need people who are used to dealing with crowds."

"And can stop any dumbasses who might wanna toboggan downstairs," added Michael.

"Okay," Anthony nodded. "That's number one: better security. What else can we do differently to improve the next fish fry?"

"We can play dunk the white guy." Michael laughed and nodded at Rob.

Rob laughed back. "Or the loudmouths."

"Anyone have an actual idea?" Anthony asked.

"How about a full brass band?" Michael suggested.

Anthony nodded. "We could have fireworks."

"A raffle," Michael offered.

Still nodding. "We could line up stalls and start selling things."

"We could charge vendors for booth space!" Michael crowed; now it was a competition.

Rob was watching, leaning into their huddle, visibly eager to see what Anthony might suggest next. If he had been any less excited, he might have heard the door open behind them. Same for Michael and Anthony. But none of them noticed Renee standing with her arms crossed until the words struck like lightning from her mouth.

"Is this some kind of joke?"

No one said anything.

So Renee filled the silence. "Am I really listening to you two idiots talking about *another* fish fry when people were *literally* jumping in and out of the house?"

"Carter didn't actually make it out of the house …" Anthony shouldn't have said. "So technically, that didn't count."

Renee glared at Anthony long enough to make him squirm, then a few seconds longer to cast that same pall upon his company.

Then she continued. "Your little party ended with an *ambulance*. I cannot think of a reason *any* of you would even consider that bullshit again. Have you had this conversation with Riley?"

She turned her unflinching gaze upon Rob.

But Rob wasn't nearly as strong, mumbling as he looked down at the floor. "No."

"It wasn't a *little* party." Again he shouldn't have said it, but Anthony kept on going. "Sure, we had a few hiccups, but people had *fun*. Everyone was excited. They're *still* excited. And best of all, we made over a thousand bucks on the fry."

"So. You're telling me that we need to do that fifty times before we can—"

"Of course not." Anthony shook his head, ignoring the raging aching inside it. "We need to get better. Think of this as a pilot. We just set everything up; now we can keep improving it."

"He's right," Michael interjected. "We could do five times what we did this last time if we plan right."

Rob found his courage. "Riley did have a lot of fun at both of the fries, and she's looking for anything that might help save the neighborhood. This fish fry idea really does have a shot."

Mentioning Riley had been the right move. Anthony could see Renee relenting. "But you'll need better security. And more fryers. And weather insurance ..." She stopped itemizing the list on her fingers at the sound of scratching on the front door.

The dog from last night had been standing on its hind legs with its paws pressed to the door, so a bundle of fur was suddenly sailing forward into the house. It bounded back onto its feet, then ran in yipping circles around Renee until she got down on her knees and ran a hand through its fur.

The dog was like a bag of candy to Renee, so Anthony was hoping for a smile, but instead, she looked up at him with an expression that triggered an involuntary shudder.

"Anyone know who that doggy belongs to?" Anthony asked.

"That 'doggy' is a local stray," Michael replied, making fun of his cousin.

"How do you know?" Renee asked him, turning from Anthony.

"Keith was asking around about it last night. He thinks it was probably left behind when one of the homes got foreclosed on."

"Come on, Fry Guy. Let's get you some food."

Renee walked toward the kitchen, and Fry Guy followed.

"That dog doesn't belong to us, you know!" Anthony called out behind her.

"Right now, I like him better than you," Renee replied.

Michael laughed. "So, I guess you gotta dog now."

Chapter Fifteen

ANTHONY'S EGGS were delicious as usual, but there was an awful lot of clanking silverware, and even two days later, the conversation still felt like stepping on shells.

"These are really good," said Renee, after swallowing another forkful of eggs.

She offered a stiff smile, and Anthony smiled back.

"So Michael said he was going out to handle some business for the next fish fry, but he didn't tell you what that business was?"

A long beat as Renee swallowed an especially generous bite, then a self-conscious laugh followed by, "Right." Then again: "These are really good."

"Thank you for booking my doctor's appointment. I really appreciate it."

This time she replied before eating more eggs. "Well, I really appreciate you finally going."

"I wouldn't be going if you hadn't made the appointment ... we both know I was dragging my ass on that."

"Yes. You were." Renee smiled, then she set down her fork and placed her hand over Anthony's. "But you're not anymore. It doesn't matter how you got the appointment. It matters that you're going. You want us to live a long life together? Then you need to start taking better care of yourself."

They stared into one another's eyes, tasting the moment even more than their eggs, lingering until they both laughed at the unlikely sight outside their window: Miss Adelaide stopping Jonah on the road and straightening his hair.

"You can't go out looking like that!" Anthony declared in an admirable impression of Miss Adelaide. "I need to help you look more presentable."

"But I'm fine like this," Anthony protested, now inhabiting Jonah.

"You're not fine! You look sloppy!" Anthony continued with an aside: "*Now imagine she just whacked him on the side of his head.* 'You know sloppy won't get you anywhere!'"

"But I get straight A's, Miss Adelaide!"

"A is the second letter in *failure*, young man!" Anthony finished as their favorite cantankerous old neighbor, grabbing his glass to wet his dry mouth.

Renee was laughing, and it felt like he'd just won a prize. "When are you going to start writing all those stories you keep in your head?"

Anthony offered his usual answer. "Maybe someday."

He could see in her eyes that she was hoping for more, but when it came to his writing, that wasn't a place where he had any more to give her. At least not yet.

So Anthony stood and walked over to her side of the table and offered what he could, kneeling down and taking her hands in his, then addressing the genuine issue.

"Thank you for supporting me in the fish fry. I promise, baby, it'll be worth it for our neighborhood."

Her eyes had softened, despite her begrudging words. "Well, it's worth it for me if it's worth it for you." Then she wiggled her hands out from under his grip and placed one on each side of his face. "You better tell me what the doctor says. You're a hell of a lot more important to me than any home."

Anthony answered without any words, still staring into her eyes.

"Thanks for that." She finally blinked. "Now, get to work. We wouldn't want Scott Hodson to get a bug up his butt on this fine Monday morning."

He gave her a kiss, then finished getting ready for work.

Ten minutes later, Anthony was getting into the Wrangler, not just thinking about Renee and how important their relationship was to him but realizing in a way that he hadn't before how much she was sacrificing by supporting this next fish fry.

Renee clearly didn't like the idea, but Anthony had been downplaying her resistance and the subsequent disappointment resulting from a second event that had spiraled (ever so slightly) out of control.

But there he was, doing the same thing again.

It hadn't spiraled *ever so slightly out of control.* Like she said, their shindig had ended with an ambulance. Renee kept repeating the same thing in different words, but her missives had fallen on mostly deaf ears.

Maybe he *should* consider calling this third fish fry off. After all, Renee was more important than any neighborhood.

Anthony swung into the ContentHive parking lot, still turning the pros and cons in his head as he pulled into a spot seven spaces away and across from Kevin. He imagined what his friend and coworker might say about all of this.

Five minutes later, he found out that he wasn't too far off at all.

"That shit was phenomenal," said Kevin, setting a steaming cup of coffee next to Anthony. "Part of me was like, *Dude, slow down on the drinking.* But the rest of me was like, *Shut up, you're drunk!*"

Anthony lifted his head from the desk and looked over at Kevin. "I do *not* want to be here today."

"I wouldn't want to be at work either if I lived with the fish like you do."

"I don't 'live with the fish.' That doesn't even make sense."

"You live in the casa de la fiesta, bro. Home of the most epic fish fry in history."

Anthony shook his head. "That was *not* the most epic fish fry in history."

"Great." Kevin grinned. "How are we going to top it?"

"We're—" Anthony stopped and turned to his screen, spotting Scott Hodson coming out of his office a full two seconds before the boss saw him.

Kevin followed his lead.

Hodson sidled up behind them and stood there like a creeper as Anthony imagined the litany of one-liners Kevin must be composing in his head.

"Any fresh angles for Mow Me Down you'd like to share?" Hodson finally asked.

"Um, no, sir," Anthony replied. "I'm just focused on saying the same things in as many different ways as I can. But no fresh angles … you either want a nice lawn, or you don't."

"Interesting …" said Scott Hodson, in a voice that

suggested the opposite. "I could say the same thing about your paycheck, you either get it, or you don't."

Hodson gave the moment a long pause, surely intended to make his subordinate squirm, but instead, Anthony used it to remind himself what a giant turd his boss actually was.

"I would work on finding a few fresh angles if you still want that paycheck," Hodson finally finished before walking off.

"Like he could ever really fire you," Kevin said once the dork was out of earshot.

"Oh, he could fire me," Anthony replied.

"But he wouldn't. Because then he'd have to do all of your work. And even though he would never admit it out loud, Scott Hodson totally knows he sucks. Think about it; there's no way that dude has ever been on a date without the girl telling him how hard he sucks at the end of it. I bet half of them say they're going to the bathroom before they even order and never come back."

Anthony shook his head but didn't respond.

Kevin finally got to business. Sort of. "You want help thinking up some 'fresh angles' that aren't Hodson's shit ones that he seems to have forgotten came from him in the first place? Maybe—"

"Would you rather talk about lawn care or our next fish fry?"

"I'm crazy with ideas, so fish fry it is," Kevin replied.

"You're crazy, *period*. Like what?"

"We should sell our *I Quit!* shirts at the fry."

"I love that idea … we could have all kinds of merch … T-shirts, novelty tumblers, Fish Fry luges …" Anthony smiled, wide and then wider. He finally started laughing out loud. He bit his lip to stop and hopefully keep Scott Hodson from coming back over.

"What's up, chuckles?" Kevin asked.

"I thought of the perfect slogan."

"What is it?"

"Something so good, my kid'll be saying it one day," Anthony crowed.

Kevin nodded. "That's an amazing Scott Hodson impression."

"Well, you know that saying, Life's a bitch and then you die …" Anthony smiled again.

And this time, Kevin couldn't hide his admiration, immediately seeing the tweak Anthony was making to the phrase and laughing along with his buddy as they repeated the slogan together.

Life's a fish, and then you fry.

Chapter Sixteen

ANTHONY SAT AT HIS DESK, more focused on his work than he'd been before at any other time during his tenure at ContentHive. He needed to finish for the day, seeing as he'd be leaving for his appointment with the specialist in a few minutes, and maybe get his raging headaches taken care of once and for all.

Unfortunately for Scott Hodson, Anthony's work today had nothing to do with lawn care, toilet paper, or any of the other products he couldn't care enough to write copy about. He and Kevin had been volleying ideas all morning, and his enthusiasm for the third fish fry was now rolling toward a boil. He hadn't forgotten Renee's objections or the desire to support his wife, but the sun was shining too brightly on what a successful event, now less than a week away, might do for their neighborhood to allow her shadows of doubt to darken the idea's potential.

So Anthony ignored that nagging voice in the back of his head and kept massaging his plan, working on a shared doc with Kevin that they kept hidden from the boss. It was usually hard to find flow while sitting at ContentHive, and yet today, his fingers barely stopped moving. Every time Anthony paused to rest, he was struck with yet another new idea.

He had just finished adding his latest brain gas to the doc — Rent port-a-potties so that the party could stay on the street and away from the houses — when his phone buzzed on the desk.

He snatched it into his hand, looked at the screen, and saw a text from Michael: *Down in the Treme is touring and might be available. We can maybe book them if we kick some serious ass. That means get your ass down here RIGHT NOW.*

There was an address, but Anthony thought it was probably best to ignore it. Michael could take care of the booking himself. He knew how much Anthony loved the band and probably wanted to give him the chance.

Down in the Treme wasn't just one of the biggest brass bands from NOLA; they were Anthony's *favorite*. Having them play at the fish fry would be a dream come true.

Renee loved the band, too. Booking them might get her more on board.

In fact, it probably would.

No. *Of course, it would.*

Sure, she would be upset that he missed his doctor's appointment, but such a thing could always be rescheduled. That wasn't true when it came to a golden moment like this one.

His headaches were a concern, but booking Down in the Treme was an opportunity with a ticking clock that Anthony couldn't ignore.

Plus, the fish fry was now a priority. Kevin had come up with some incredible logo designs, and it was getting harder and harder to think about anything else.

If he missed out on booking Treme, it wouldn't just feel

like he was failing the fish fry. It would feel like Anthony was failing himself.

Even after all these years, the memories were ripe: Grandma taking him to Opelousas to see Down in the Treme when he was just a boy. Of course, the band would have different members now, but it still felt like a sign from above, telling Anthony to go ahead with the fish fry: *full steam ahead.*

Anthony sighed, knowing what he had to do, then turned off his computer and slid the chair away from his desk.

"Off to your doctor's appointment?" Kevin asked.

"Something like that." Anthony grinned as he stood.

"Where do you think you're going?" Of course, Scott Hodson was suddenly there, and of course, the jerk had already forgotten that Anthony was scheduled to leave early today.

"To a doctor's appointment. Like I told you."

"Right." Hodson nodded. "Because there weren't any appointments available at a time that didn't interfere with your workday."

"It's a doctor's office. What did you want me to do?"

"Is your work done for the day?"

"Of course, it is," Anthony lied.

"Well then, good luck at your appointment, I guess. Maybe you should make one at the barbershop next. Finally, take care of the dreaded dreads."

"They're locs," Anthony tried not to growl as he passed the boss on his way out.

He got into his Wrangler, checked the address, then drove to a rehearsal studio on Euclid Street, careful not to speed like his bursting excitement wanted him to.

He could hear the music as he parked, and the beat got his heart pumping harder than it already was. He slammed the Jeep door, smiling wide as he practically skipped down the sidewalk, opening the door to a nostalgic blast of brass-infused music that reached right inside to squeeze his soul.

Down in the Treme was in full form, playing a roof-rattling rendition of "Do What You Wanna." No one noticed Anthony as he entered. Not even Michael, dancing and clapping along with the band, his body as alive as Anthony's spirit, almost overwhelmed by the joy he felt at hearing so much Louisiana in their sound.

Michael finally spied him several moments later, but the song was still going. It sounded like the music was about to stop several times, but the notes kept blasting for another ten minutes or so before reaching an uproarious finish, full of crashing cymbals and exuberant brass.

Michael looked over at Anthony and told him not to mess this up without having to say a thing — the set of his eyes was plenty loud enough. A giant of a man kept pace beside him, a full head taller than Anthony and at least twice as wide.

"Elijah, Anthony. Anthony, Elijah." Michael nodded from one man to the other. "Elijah is Treme's newest band-leader. Anthony is the man who is just *absolutely dying* to have you all play at his fish fry."

Elijah vented a long and hearty laugh. "The final Friday of Lent, am I right?"

Anthony nodded.

"Well then, you lucky we got space. We was gonna play another gig, but it got canceled. I already talked to the boys. Told 'em we could either book this or finish our tour early and head back home."

Anthony smiled. "I vote you book this."

"I don't know." Another laugh. "NOLA is calling."

"Come to our fish fry, and you'll feel like you're back home already," Anthony promised.

"We'll need full payment up front."

"Not a problem," Michael said before Anthony could interject.

"How much will it cost to book you?" Anthony asked.

"Four grand," Elijah said with a decisive nod.

"Not a problem," Michael repeated.

"Actually …" Anthony laughed, but his little chuckle held none of the band leader's earlier merriment. "That might be a problem."

Michael shook his head, turning from Anthony and addressing Elijah. "We got this."

"Do you?" Elijah asked.

Anthony gestured to the band, then looked right into Elijah's eyes. "Would you mind giving me and my cousin a moment to speak? Believe me, man, I love what you guys do and would love nothing more than to have you play at the fish fry. One of my earliest and most favorite memories is seeing you guys play when I was a kid. A bunch of times, actually. But the best was at Opelousas when I was eleven. Back when Emmanuel Saint was still playing with the band. I heard a version of "Heebie Jeebies" that day that hasn't left me since. So, I'd love to have you at the fish fry more than anything, and sure as hell appreciate your time and how many musicians you support at that price, but I've gotta make sure we can cover the cost without sacrificing something that's equally or maybe even more important."

Elijah gave Anthony a broad smile and clapped him on the shoulder. "That just sounds like smart business, son. You give it a think and let me know what you decide."

Another smile, and then Elijah walked away.

"The hell, man?" Michael was already on him. "You really complaining about the price of—"

"I'm not complaining about anything. But I can't make money out of nowhere."

"Did you lose all your credit cards?"

"I have five grand left on my credit card, *max*. And if we're really doing this, I have to make sure I do it right. That means security and weather insurance."

"*Weather insurance*?" Michael laughed.

"Yes, weather insurance. Maybe you don't care if we lose our ass on this event, but seeing as I'd like to stay married, *I do*."

"There ain't gonna be no rain, man!" Michael huffed, waving his hands in irritation. "The weather will be good. It's *always* good. And even if it's not, folks in Atlanta know how to have fun in a little rain. Are you really such a little bitch that you're willing to drop four grand on insurance but not on booking your favorite brass band for a memory you can carry for the rest of your life?"

"You're an asshole," Anthony said.

"Because I'm right?"

"Maybe."

"You know I am. Now, are you gonna go for the band or not?"

Anthony hesitated. How likely was it that it would rain? And when would he ever have the chance to have *Down in the Treme* at his own event again? "Okay, let's do this."

"If you've got 5K on that credit card, I suggest we add fireworks to the tab." Michael didn't wait for an answer, raising his hand and waving Elijah back over to their huddle. "A thousand dollars' worth oughta do it."

Chapter Seventeen

"MAN, you've *got* to stop worrying," Michael said from the passenger seat.

"And you've *got* to stop telling me to stop worrying. Do I look worried?"

"I don't know. Does this look worried to you?" Michael pinched his face in a way that made his expression appear melted more than disquieted, but Anthony pretended that he couldn't see it in his peripheral vision.

"I'm driving. I can't look at you being a dumbass right now."

"I know you can see me looking like you." Michael made his voice a falsetto. "Oh no! I'm so worried my lady's gonna spank me for not getting insurance." He shook his head, laughing. "Tell me I'm wrong."

"You're wrong."

"You're really trying to say you ain't worried about what Renee's gonna say about you booking a brass band instead of buying insurance?"

"YOU TOLD ME TO BOOK THE BAND!"

"Watch. I'm gonna tell you to jump off a bridge just to

see what happens." Then: "So, you *are* worried about Renee."

"I'm happy that we booked the band. I'm *excited* we booked the band."

"I notice you didn't answer my question."

"She won't be pissed that I booked the band so much as I missed my doctor's appointment to meet them," Anthony replied after a lingering pause.

"Man, you need Viagra, just get it off the internet."

"For my headaches."

"All the pharmacies out of Tylenol?"

Anthony shook his throbbing head, ignoring his cousin as he swung onto Edgewood.

Michael pointed at Rob, running across the street, waving his phone and shouting. "Why is Barney running over here like a big white rhino?"

"His name is Rob," Anthony corrected.

"Like I don't know Barney's name."

Anthony waved at a frantic-looking Rob as he pulled into his driveway.

He shouted as he ran over. "I just got off the phone with Lenny Burns!"

"You were talking to Lenny Burns?" Michael sounded both impressed and incredulous. "Why did he want to talk to you?"

"I wasn't talking to *him*," Rob explained, with a note of disappointment in himself. "I was talking to someone at the Lenny Burns Show. And they don't care about me. They wanted to talk to *you*."

Rob nodded at Anthony.

"Me?" Anthony pointed at his chest.

"Lenny need some advice on how to look goofy?" Michael asked.

"They want to talk about the fish fry! I sent them

pictures from the last one; a friend of a friend had their email address. And they actually got back to me! So I told them about trying to save the neighborhood and that you were bringing your grandma's Louisiana Fish Fry to Atlanta," Rob announced, generating enough excitement to power a lamp. "They want to interview you, but it has to be *right now*."

Anthony was flabbergasted. "What do I say?"

"He's not ready." Michael shook his head. "I'll do it."

"Just be yourself," Rob assured him. "That's what you're best at."

"Renee says I'm best at making a mess or making shit up. So when is this supposed to happen?"

"I told you, *right now*."

Anthony looked around. "Where's Lenny?"

Rob shook his phone in the air. "He's calling me back."

"He can't call you back if you've never talked to him," Michael argued.

"Cool. Let me check in with Renee and—"

"Don't leave. He's calling right back."

"Again …" Michael said.

"I'll just be a—"

Rob's phone rang in his hand. He offered it to Anthony.

It was do or die, and he had no other choice. He swallowed and took the phone.

"This is Anthony Joyner."

"ANTHONY JOYNER!" Lenny repeated in a booming (syndicated) voice. "I just read your blog post and must admit to being blown away by your passion, man. Can you tell our listeners what was it that made you want to bring a little Louisiana here to Georgia?"

Anthony's chest filled with pride at the question. He

was doing something bold, embracing his neighborhood and trying to save it. Of course, he wanted to crow about it.

"I guess it was two things at once. I grew up a small-town Louisiana boy with a grandma who worshiped food only slightly less than she worshiped the Lord. Fish fries were her favorite, and that made them something I always looked forward to all through my childhood. I've been missing my grandmother since before she had to move in with my aunt in Texas for full-time care in her old age, but lately, I've also been longing for a little bit of Louisiana myself."

Anthony was already talking loudly into the phone, but as his neighbors crowded around him, he got even louder.

"At first, we just wanted to bring some of our old home into the new place, but we all had so much fun with the first one, we decided to do it again, but with a mission."

He grinned for the crowd, then waited for Lenny to return his volley.

"And would you mind telling us more about your mission?" Lenny asked.

"Well, let's just say it's more of a 'mission critical' than a 'mission impossible.'"

Anthony laughed, slipping deeper into what felt like a natural role. He looked around for Renee, hoping she might come out to investigate whatever was happening out in the street ... or maybe just to see why her husband had pulled into the driveway without coming inside.

"A neighborhood thrives thanks to its community, and old communities are constantly threatened by new waves of gentrification. I couldn't stand the thought of seeing my neighborhood roots ripped up from the ground just so the surrounding land can get planted with a fresh crop of quickly climbing property values."

Anthony barely knew where all that had come from. He looked around at his neighbors — several now sitting in their cars with the windows down, cranking Big Lenny from their speakers, so the broadcast rolled through the cul-de-sac like a gentle rumble of thunder through the sky.

He stood even straighter and finished. "It's up to us to save our neighborhood! But there's no reason we can't have a helluva lot of fun doing it."

"Tell 'em about the desserts," Jonah shouted.

"And the Jell-O shots," Ezekiel added.

"Hush now." Miss Adelaide waved all the neighbors down as they clamored to share the best parts of the fish fry with their favorite radio host. "Let the man speak."

And Anthony did, with more confidence than he would have thought possible just five minutes ago. Lenny finished the interview with a short queue of questions, prompting Anthony to cover more of the *who*, *what*, *where*, and *why* of the upcoming fry. And finally, as Big Lenny cut to commercial break, a collective cheer erupted in the cul-de-sac.

Anthony might as well have been holding a hundred balloons in each hand. He turned to his front porch, hoping that Renee was finally outside, wanting and needing her to see this. He grinned when she saw her.

But the expression on her face was far from a smile.

She exhaled hard enough for him to see it, then turned around and went inside the house.

Anthony felt like he'd been shaken upside down by the ankles and all emptied out.

Every one of his two hundred balloons was now deflated, but he kept standing straight and held his smile as the boisterous crowd closed in around him.

Chapter Eighteen

ANTHONY DID his best to acknowledge the neighbors while keeping things brief.

"The hell is wrong with you?" Michael asked, talking a mile a minute, seemingly convinced that he and his cousin were newly anointed gods of the fish fry. Anthony didn't answer, so Michael raised a fist and pumped it in the air, hollering on their way to the porch. "ATLANTA FISH FRY!"

But Anthony couldn't help his apprehension. He didn't know for sure what might be waiting on the other side of his front door, but he wasn't a stranger to that sour expression he'd seen on his wife's face.

He couldn't figure out if it was the missed doctor's appointment, the fish fry expanding its reach, or (the worst option of all) that she'd already found out about the weather insurance money going to the band.

"Seriously," Michael tried again as he opened the door, with Anthony still a long and tentative step behind him. "What's up, man?"

"Nothing," Anthony said.

"It's something," Michael huffed. A beat, then, "You in trouble with the Mrs.?"

"No, I'm not 'in trouble with the Mrs." But in truth, Anthony was totally in trouble with the Mrs. He could feel her irritation (at best) or anger (at worst) before he entered the kitchen to see her scrubbing the dishes with a grudge.

Renee must have heard them come in behind her, but she didn't turn around.

Michael gave him a knowing look, silently ridiculing his cousin with a smile and nod that said plenty: *See like I said, you're in trouble with the Mrs!*

"Hey, baby," Anthony tried.

No response from Renee, so Michael walked over to the sink and stood right beside her. "Everything okay?"

She stopped washing, turned off the water, then spun around, looking past Michael at Anthony. "No. I am not okay. Fry Guy has gone missing."

Anthony felt buoyed by a moment of hope — maybe she wasn't mad at him after all.

"That's not even our dog!" He added a little laugh at the end of his comment, but judging by her glare, both were mistakes.

"How about I go and look for him?" Michael offered, likely wanting to avoid whatever was happening in the kitchen as much as he cared to help. "With all the food up and down this street, I can't imagine the little guy would have gone far."

"Thanks, Michael," Renee said, her glare still fixed on Anthony.

"No problem." He nodded, then flashed another glance at his cousin: *Good luck, man.*

Anthony gave Renee a tentative smile as Michael left.

But she didn't smile back.

"What's wrong?" he asked. "Because I know it's not the dog."

"I am upset about the dog, Anthony." Renee crossed her arms.

He waited through a long and awkward moment of silence, knowing she hadn't finished her thought.

Then finally: "How did your doctor's appointment go?"

Shit. Crap. Dammit.

"I had to reschedule."

Renee raised her eyebrows and repeated his bullshit. "You had to reschedule?"

"Something came up."

And again, she repeated his bullshit. "Something came up …"

He was chewing on his next response when Renee made things harder. "Is there a chance that you didn't reschedule? And that maybe you just *didn't show up?*"

"What makes you say that?" Like his heart wasn't pounding.

She shook her head, disgusted. "Maybe I know it because I took time out of my busy day to support you, Anthony. But you couldn't even do the bare minimum by showing up to the appointment that *I had to make for you.* I wanted to be there for you; instead, I spent an hour waiting at that doctor's office by myself and worrying while—"

"You could have just texted. I would have—"

"What did you say?" Her voice was sharp enough to cut through a steel cable.

"Nothing." He shook his head. "I'll reschedule."

"I'm sure you will."

"I promise."

"You talk *such* a good game, but you only *do* what you think is beneficial for you."

"I'm really sorry, Renee. I've just had so much on my mind lately—"

"No shit, Anthony! But you focus on all the wrong things!"

He chewed his bottom lip for a beat before responding. Renee was right to be upset with him for missing his doctor's appointment and dragging ass on making it in the first place, but it wasn't right to discount his efforts at saving the neighborhood.

"That's not fair." Anthony shook his head without even attempting to argue his point further, really not wanting to fight.

But he'd apparently pushed it too far already, and Renee wasn't about to let it go.

"What part isn't fair, Anthony?"

"I'm trying to save the neighborhood … and it would be nice if you saw that and supported me."

"SUPPORT YOU?" She drew a deep breath, probably to keep herself from breaking a plate over his head, then, in a much softer voice, she said, "I've done nothing *but* support you, Anthony. I've believed in you, and I've stood by you, but this has finally gone too far."

What do you mean? he wanted to ask.

Anthony might not have managed to gather the courage, but Renee didn't even give him a chance.

"This whole fish fry business is insane."

"It's not a business. It's an attempt to—"

"You can't save this neighborhood, Anthony! Half of it is already sold, and the rest will be gone in a month." She looked a hiccup away from some serious tears. "You're just using this situation as an excuse to stick your head in the sand and avoid what *actually* matters."

She was getting increasingly upset, her voice rising in

pitch and volume, vacillating between what sounded like anger and sorrow.

"I'm not putting my head in the sand," he tried to argue.

But she still wasn't having it. "You can't just say things you want to be true out loud and then expect them to actually be true." She shook her head, then walked past him and out of the kitchen.

He followed her into the living room.

But she stopped short, turning back to Anthony. "I can't be with a man who is so willing to ignore his health, even after his wife *begs* him to do something about it."

"It's just headaches."

"*Just headaches?*" Her voice went eerily calm. "I see you every day, Anthony. It's not *just headaches*, and you know it. Something is wrong, and you refuse to even acknowledge it."

"I promise, I'm—" Anthony stopped, his heart refusing to beat. He exhaled, then drew another breath. "You can't be serious …"

He pointed to her suitcase, resting by the front door with her jacket draped atop it, presumably already packed.

Renee said, "I told you I'd be leaving if you didn't take care of yourself, but you refused to believe me."

"I didn't refuse to believe you."

"Really?" She looked him up and down. "Because that's not what it looks like from this side of the conversation."

"Please … we don't have to do this. Couldn't we just—"

"No, Anthony. We can't 'just' anything. Not right now. Not until you figure a few things out."

"Just give me a second chance. I get it now. It won't

happen again. There must be *something* I can do! Please ... I'll do anything."

Anthony stared into her eyes, waiting for Renee to finally soften.

But apparently, this time, he'd pushed her too far.

"You want to do something?" She didn't wait for his answer. "Tell Michael he can bring Fry Guy to my mom's house if he finds him."

"Fry Guy?"

"That's right, Anthony. Fry Guy. I could really use somebody to love right now that will love me back."

"That's not fair ... you know I love you ..."

"Love me in the way I need to be loved right now." She grabbed her jacket and suitcase, then opened the front door.

"We can fix this. Not just this thing with us, but everything. I'll make an appointment for the soonest I can get one, even if it means taking more time off work and dealing with Hodson. And as for the neighborhood—"

"The neighborhood is *gone*, Anthony." The first tear finally slid down her cheek as she delivered the final blow. "Aunt Ida called about an hour ago. She's sold the house to Eddison Fisher."

Chapter Nineteen

ANTHONY WAS on his third circuit of the empty house when he heard the front door open.

It was Michael at the door, not Renee. Even when angry, she had a lighter gait, with an unmistakable tone of spitfire energy. Michael was a small man who stomped around as though thunderous steps might lend him an inch.

So off to the bathroom he went. He sat on the closed toilet, forehead cradled in his broad palms, with what felt like an icepick buried in his skull. He sighed, wishing he'd handled things better. The only thing worse than Renee being mad at him was … nothing.

"You jerking off in there?" Michael asked from the other side of the door.

Anthony ignored him, standing from the toilet to grab the handful of Advil he should have taken as soon as he entered the bathroom. Or before.

Renee was right — what the hell was wrong with him? Why did he keep refusing to take care of himself?

A soft knock at the door. "You need any help? If you

don't got your phone on you, I could maybe tell you a dirty story. Want the details about what happened after I stole Candace from right under your nose outside Popeye's? The story ends back at my place with her—"

"I'm not in the mood," Anthony said as he opened the bathroom door.

"Oh, man. You look like my butthole feels after chili. You need a laxative or something?"

"I told you, I'm not in the mood."

"And I told you, your face looks like the emotional money shot in a Pixar movie."

Anthony shook his head, walking back toward the living room. "You're saying things that have nothing in common."

"You deaf? They're both about how you look like shit."

Anthony sat on the couch. "You implied that I look hot and irritated before suggesting I was constipated. Then you said I look sad."

"Dumbass." Michael shook his head. "They have everything in common. You look like shit because you're emotionally constipated, and that makes you look like the guy about to go postal in a movie."

"And which movie is this?" He so wasn't in the mood, but Anthony did his best to fake a smile, not wanting to discuss the situation or bring his cousin down.

But that was just something else for him to fail at.

Michael said, "Seriously, man. I can cancel my plans with Lacy and stay home with you."

"You should totally go." Then, in case that made him sound like a jerk, "I mean, I'm fine. For real."

"You don't look fine."

"That's because you're still here." Anthony laughed.

"Why don't you leave, then we can both see how happy I am."

"How'm I supposed to see you if I ain't even here?"

"I'll send you a selfie." Anthony laughed again, but he still wasn't feeling it. "Seriously, go on, man. I know she's your one-that-got-away."

"Now I know you're fine. You're spouting your usual bullshit."

But Michael didn't press any further. Instead, he left Anthony to his ample regret, telling him he'd be back in an hour or so.

"We can drive up to Back to the Bayou and do what the brobots couldn't."

Anthony didn't reply, sitting on the couch for another quarter-hour after Michael left while taking inventory of the many ways he could have handled the situation with Renee better.

Then he finally got off the couch and went into the kitchen for something to eat. There was a nice piece of fish in the fridge, and he would have happily eaten it for dinner if his stomach hadn't lurched at the sight.

So he made himself a peanut butter and jelly sandwich instead, eating it alone at his kitchen table, slowly chewing, as if the longer he took to finish, the better he might feel by the end of it.

But the languorous speed wasn't helping. The PB&J did little to curb his hunger, and with one half of it now gone and the other half down to crusts, he wondered what he could do to make things better with Renee.

You could start by calling the doctor and rescheduling that appointment, said a nagging voice inside him.

His raging headache agreed.

Anthony planned to make the call right after he finished his sandwich, but then he caught a glint from the corner of his eye as he was standing. He took his plate to the sink and went to investigate.

He found a shard of glass from the last fry, something broken that had escaped the cleanup. It hardly made up for all that had gone wrong between him and Renee, but at least when he was down on all fours cleaning, he felt like less of an ass. Same for when he started scrubbing the sticky spot beneath it.

True to his word, Michael returned an hour or so later. He rapped on the door with the heel of his fist, same as he had since they were kids, but he didn't enter. Instead, he waited for Anthony to answer the door. And when he didn't, Michael opened up and yelled into the living room.

"WE'RE WAITING IN THE WRANGLER!"

Anthony wanted to know who else was waiting to make it a *we* and how Michael had the keys to his Jeep. But instead of bellowing his questions, he went outside and saw his cousin sitting behind the wheel, with all three bros packed into the back.

"So, I guess you're driving." Anthony climbed into the passenger seat and slammed the door.

"Sorry about last time," Jonah said as Michael backed out of the driveway.

"You don't have to apologize anymore." Anthony shook his head without turning around to look at the bros. "I get it."

After a few moments of silence, Jonah tried something else. "We called ahead to order everything."

"We're gonna do it up right this time!" Michael announced, excitement in full swing even if his cousin was stuck in a lull.

"We need music," Carter suggested.

"What do you like?" Michael reached for the radio. "John Mayer? Three Doors Down?"

133

Anthony laughed, and for the first time, it felt genuine. "Maroon 5 for sure."

But the CD player was on instead of the radio, and Outkast was already loaded, so Michael let "Bombs Over Baghdad" keep playing.

Everyone was happy and laughing along with the music. Anthony might have felt better enough to join them, but his head was throbbing so hard that he could barely see through the windshield. And the exhaustion was getting to him. It was like he'd been operating on borrowed energy, and now that Renee was gone, the piper had suddenly called in the loan.

His stomach was suddenly catching up with his headache. He began breathing in and out, controlling his inhales and exhales, trying not to think about what might—

"PULL OVER!" Anthony yelled.

Michael looked over, alarmed, then wrenched the wheel to the right and sent the Wrangler flying two lanes over to the side of the road.

Anthony opened his door and scrambled out of the Jeep, making it four strides before doubling over and spilling liquid anxiety onto the sidewalk.

He heard another door open as he kept on vomiting, followed by the sound of Michael's definitive march to Anthony's side of the Wrangler.

"You okay, man?" Michael slapped a hand on his back.

"I'm good," he said, standing straight.

"This a headache thing or a Renee thing?"

"I think it's both." Anthony wiped his lips, wishing for something to drink so he could wash the sourness out of his mouth. Like a good friend and mindreader, Michael handed him a bottle of water.

"Thanks," Anthony said, taking a sip.

"It's mostly backwash."

Anthony shrugged, wishing he had it in him to laugh. "Delicious."

"So, you finally calling that specialist? Or you need another wife to leave you?"

"I'll call as soon as we get home," Anthony said, meaning every word.

Michael handed him a phone. "Just press *Send*."

Anthony looked down at the screen in confusion, then back up at his cousin.

"Renee gave me the number," Michael explained. "She also gave me an earful about how to take care of family."

Anthony nodded and made the call, first apologizing for missing his prior appointment before promising not to miss this next one.

The receptionist started out cold, then warmed to his sincerity and found a cancelation spot for him just two days from now. She signed off, telling him to have a great day. Though it still felt like a tall order, for the first time since his celebration in the street had finished — about twenty minutes before Renee had walked out on him — it at least felt like a distinct possibility.

Anthony ended the call and got back into the Jeep.

"So ... we going to Bayou?" Michael asked with his hands on the wheel.

But Anthony shook his head. "Let's go home. For right now, Louisiana can wait."

He expected Michael to start making fun of him.

Instead, his cousin turned the Wrangler around.

Chapter Twenty

IT WAS ALWAYS hard for Anthony to show up for a job he could barely stand, but with a raging headache and a life crumbling like breading off fish, it had never been harder than this morning.

He wanted to call Renee before work, but even if she answered, he wouldn't know what to say. Any conversation would have to wait until he could tell her that he'd finally gone to the specialist he'd been promising to visit for too long.

He filled the French press with some aromatic Kenyan, but that only made him feel lonely. Even lonelier when he saw how much coffee was still in the press once he finished his cup.

He drank it all, hoping to dull the growing ache inside him. But like his headache, that only made everything worse.

He got dressed and looked out the window before leaving the house, determined to avoid Joy Jones on his way to the Jeep. He made it into the Wrangler without interruption, then gunned the engine and throttled his sorrow while backing out of the driveway, keeping it in check as he passed the patchy lawns and boarded windows, his gaze tracking Wendall racing down the street, yelling after one of the bros.

Twenty minutes later, Anthony was surprised to find himself pulling into the ContentHive parking lot, barely remembering his trip to get there. The writing was easy enough when he cared about what he was putting on the page, but Anthony could feel the day's struggle as he killed the engine and spent several lingering moments drawing deep breaths, slowly psyching himself up enough to head inside.

He stopped at the coffee station and grabbed a third cup that he didn't need and would probably worsen his headache, then took his seat, feeling barely human.

Kevin disagreed. "You look like shit."

"Just trying to copy your smell," Anthony replied with no emotion.

Kevin nodded, looking over at his buddy with an expression that resembled concern. "Speaking of copy, are you planning on getting to those lawn care emails today?"

"Probably not," Anthony admitted.

Kevin nodded again. "As in, you're 'probably not' going to be working here anymore if you don't get them done?"

"That's great." He laughed, but there was still no emotion.

"What's great?" Kevin asked, sounding suspicious.

"Your Scott Hodson impression." Anthony nodded, eyes on the screen as he pulled up some of his windows from the last time he was sitting down at his computer — all related to the fish fry, of course.

"Dude ... I'm just trying to help."

"I know … sorry …" Anthony shook his head. "It's me."

Kevin laughed. "Well, I didn't think it was me!"

"I don't know when the last time I was in this bad of a mood."

"Easy. It was when Ron took complete credit for your presentation that won a six-million-dollar contract."

Anthony shook his head again. "This is different."

"Anything you want to talk about?"

"Maybe later. Definitely not right now."

"Want me to write the emails for you?" asked Kevin.

"Cool of you to offer, but I've got it."

Kevin glanced at Anthony's cornucopia of open windows. "Doesn't look like it."

"This is called foreshadowing." Anthony still couldn't manage a smile.

He turned back to his laptop and closed all the windows. He stared at the blinking cursor on his new article *What About Weeds?* before shaking his head and opening WordPress to start a new blog post, the first since his laptop had died.

Anthony felt flow like he hadn't in months, his fingers blazing as he finished a passionate article about the importance of food and community, tradition, and most of all, Louisiana.

Scott Hodson was suddenly standing behind him. "Am I looking at what I think I'm looking at?"

Anthony already knew how this was about to go down. So he ignored his pounding heart and pressed *Publish* without even giving his work an edit, then he spun around in his chair.

"I don't know, *Scott Hodson. What* do you think you're looking at?"

"Care to explain your tone?" He was getting mad fast.

Finally, something to make Anthony feel better. "I'm not sure that explaining it would help. You never understand when I explain how marketing or copywriting are supposed to work, or when I try and explain the difference between a good idea and a bad one, so I'm not sure—"

"Do you want to get fired?"

Anthony appeared to consider it, then said, "Would you, please? That would really help me out because the unemployment is better that way, right? Because then it's your decision instead of mine?"

"You're making a mistake, Joyner."

"No," Anthony shook his head and kept going, "I've *been* making a mistake. I've made one each time I've sat here doing work that I can't ever care about because no matter how hard I try, it won't ever be appreciated. And it's not just that you don't know your job or good ideas from bad, Scott Hodson. It's that you're a terrible boss who doesn't have a clue about most things, especially when it comes to how borderline offensive your jokes are."

"My jokes are *not* offensive!" Scott Hodson snapped, finally defending himself in the dumbest possible way. "Take that back!"

"*Take that back?*" Anthony repeated, leaping up from his seat, now laughing and meaning it. "I'm out of here, Scott Hodson. I've got better things to do. Starting with finding a job where the person in charge knows how to treat people."

He grabbed his bag, shaking his head while walking by his former boss.

Hodson took him by the arm, firm but not aggressive. "Don't do anything you'll regret." Then, in a slightly softer voice, as if suddenly willing to fight for the asset that Anthony was: "Let's talk about it."

Anthony turned back around, finally seeing the barely

suppressed glee and undiluted shock glazing Kevin's face. "You know what, Scott Hodson? My locs aren't just perfectly acceptable for this job, they're dope — which means 'cool' — just in case you don't get it. If we were in a factory or a kitchen, or if my choice of hairstyle in any way posed a safety hazard, then maybe you'd have a point. But I sit in front of a computer and type all day. Having dreadlocks makes me a normal human being, and I deserve respect for my choices!"

He hadn't meant to start shouting, but Anthony's volume had gone from a six at the start of his first sentence to at least a nine by the climax.

Hodson stared at him open-mouthed before almost whispering, "You're fired."

"Thank you." Anthony grinned.

The entire office was in awe but silent as the start of an opera.

Except for Kevin, who could no longer stay in his seat and was unwilling to bottle his joy. He clapped and started jumping up and down, looking around the office in bafflement, failing to understand why everyone else was still sitting.

Hodson turned his glare on Kevin. "You're fired, too!"

"Obviously." Kevin laughed, giving him the finger, then grabbing his bag and following his buddy out of the Hive. He clapped Anthony on his back as the doors closed behind him. "Dude. You're like Jerry Maguire!"

And Anthony thought, *Did Jerry Maguire die from an aneurism?*

Chapter Twenty-One

FOUR HOURS LATER, Anthony put a hand on his knee to stop it from bouncing.

The direct order from his brain hadn't been enough. Not when Dr. Aubrey O'Brian left him feeling so nervous. It wasn't the doctor herself that had him on edge, it was all of this waiting. Too many nurses and technicians reminding him to wait for the doctor every time he asked how things were looking.

They asked him to stay to see the doctor instead of calling him with results. It couldn't be a good sign.

A bolt of lightning struck his head in the center like an exclamation on the thought.

The door opened, and Aubrey finally entered. A tall woman with thick shoulder-length black hair. Stern and serious-looking, but kind.

The doctor got right to it. "We've found a mass in your throat and a tumor in your brain, Mr. Joyner. We're going to have to run some tests."

Never once in history had a doctor ever wanted to 'run some tests' for fun.

"I hope I get an A," Anthony replied in the only way his stubborn brain would allow him, forever in search of the best perspective or punchline.

Aubrey smiled and waited; this wasn't her first time at the circus.

"What kind of mass?" Anthony asked.

"The cancerous kind."

"That can't be right. I came in for *headaches*. I'm not even sick. I just had a physical in March, and the doctor joked about how he should be doing more of whatever I'm doing." A little laugh to prove it. "They drew blood and the whole nine! I don't smoke — I don't even know a lot of smokers."

"I understand the weight of this new information." Aubrey nodded. "It's a lot to suddenly carry. But it isn't out of the blue. You've been telling yourself that you don't feel sick, but in reality, you've been having migraines for a while now. There's a serious disconnect there."

She gave him a beat of quiet to pickle in her words, then offered some more. "I'm here to answer your questions as best I can. Like I said, we need to run some tests. Your scan is being looked at by a neurosurgeon right now. We'll know whether the brain mass is malignant or benign soon."

Anthony couldn't even sigh. He was suddenly filled with an emptiness like outer space. He was on a roller-coaster at the peak of its climb, about to plummet into a purity of nothing below him.

Tears would fall any second. "Am I going to die from this?"

Another patient smile, and then her answer like a bludgeon. "We can't know until we run all the tests."

"But you're not saying no."

"I can't say no."

It was an impossible situation to accept so immediately, but in what was perhaps a desperate act of self-preservation, Anthony made a silent promise to himself:

I will beat this.

Aubrey kept talking. He understood the importance of what the doctor might be saying but couldn't focus on the details. Not that it mattered. She already told him all that she knew or was going to reveal ahead of the test results.

The nurse entered, and Aubrey stopped talking.

"Thank you, Javi." Then she opened the folder, nodded, and looked at Anthony with a half-smile. "It looks like we have some good and bad news."

"I won a bunch of cash, but now my wallet's going to hurt my butt on the way home?" He half-smiled back.

"The brain tumor is benign. You have a meningioma. It's not dangerous, but you'll have to get it checked out yearly. You'll just need a follow-up appointment."

"But?"

"But you do have throat cancer."

"I *can't* have throat cancer."

"I'm sorry, Mr. Joyner … it's further along than I'd like. We can treat this, but because we weren't able to catch it at an earlier stage, we'll have to get especially aggressive."

"What does that mean?"

"It means radiation. Monday through Friday."

The news washed through Anthony with a rush of regret. If he had only listened to Renee. "I'm an idiot."

"Be kind to yourself, Mr. Joyner."

"I should have come in earlier."

The doctor nodded. "Yes, that would have been a lot easier. But you didn't, and there's nothing you can do about it now. Kicking yourself for not coming in sooner won't change a thing. Your situation isn't nearly as dire as I'm sure it feels. We have an excellent chance of clearing this up entirely. It's not the worst prognosis I've given. Not even this week."

Aubrey offered him another smile, her warmest so far.

Anthony thanked the doctor for her candor and kindness, then left the office in a fog.

The murk stayed inside him all the way home.

He wasn't sure what to do or who to call first. And yes, there was the chance that he could die, but that wasn't even what Anthony cared about most. He couldn't stop thinking about how badly he failed Renee. He had been so careless. So thoughtless. So downright selfish. It took a doctor staring into his eyes and telling him there was a mass in his throat before he could take his wife's incessant pleas seriously.

Renee had been telling him to get tested for months, and for months he kept sticking his head in the sand and pretending that he loved all the grit in his ears.

He swung onto the cul-de-sac and saw Wendall with his sign: *Psalm 104:19: The sun knows the place of its setting.*

Anthony felt desperate to call her.

But he couldn't do that. Not now. Not when he only had terrible news to deliver.

He laughed out loud because that was better than crying. But the sound bounced against the windows of the Wrangler and came back at him like an enemy, reminding him of how alone he was right now.

He lost the first tear anyway, and of course, more were on the way.

He woke up this morning with a job and no cancer. Now he was unemployed, with plenty of time for all of the upcoming radiation. So no, he couldn't call Renee.

He pulled into his driveway and sighed with his dying engine.

He got out of the car, but instead of entering an empty

house he couldn't bear to feel lonely in, he wandered his neighborhood with purpose. Fry Guy was somewhere in the cul-de-sac, and Anthony was determined to find him.

Because then he could finally call Renee. Instead of opening with, *Guess what rhymes with 'answer'?*, she could hear Fry Guy barking in the background. Anthony could never recover the lost time or undo what he did, but he was determined to make sure that she got that damned dog.

His quest eventually led to Junkman's backyard. He shouldn't really be there, but Anthony wasn't about to knock on the door. Instead, he crept through the side yard and then into the back, where the Junkman kept an emporium of garbage compared to the tiny mercantile he set up out front. Inventory (trash) came in two kinds: piles and mountains. Some of these pillars were themed — one had old technology, from broken copiers to Ataris (two and a half, to be exact), while another boasted clothing from every photographable era, assuming photography started around the Civil War.

He managed to inspect every cluttered inch of the yard without alerting Junkman, but he still couldn't find Fry Guy anywhere. He eventually had to surrender, heading back home but still unwilling to go inside.

Anthony sat on his porch, pouting, his back pressed against the wall even though he wanted to sit on the swing one of the neighbors must have repaired since the chaotic fry.

But then someone might see him and want to come over.

He stayed incognito for another half hour, but then Michael saw him sitting there and started calling him Little Orphan Anthony before he finally got down on his ass and sat right next to him, rolling jokes like joints and passing them over until he finally got his cousin to open up.

"I lost my job," Anthony admitted.

"The one that you hate?"

"The one I can't tell Renee that I don't have anymore. At least not until I get another one. And find Fry Guy." He swallowed.

"What aren't you telling me, man?"

Anthony shook his head.

Michael waited.

And waited …

Until finally: "The specialist said I have cancer."

Michael nodded, not even making a joke as he waited for more.

Then Anthony broke down, thoroughly losing his shit as he started to cry and then sob.

Michael held him through it, letting his cousin soak a shirt that Anthony already knew from here on out would be the one that Michael insisted he had "ruined with his tears."

Anthony finally stopped crying and pulled away.

Still no jokes, but Michael didn't let him off the hook entirely. "She was right about you sticking your head in the sand."

The tears came again or would have if Anthony hadn't sucked them back in. "I'm going to cancel the fish fry."

Michael stood and offered his hand to Anthony. Once his cousin was back on his feet, he delivered yet one more nugget of terrible news on a day that had already been full of it.

"Might as well. Darius Jones just sold The Canopy and both of his houses."

"You're kidding," Anthony said.

"To Eddison Fisher," Michael finished.

Chapter Twenty-Two

THE REST of Anthony's night was so miserable that he didn't even remember how it ended. Michael tried to cheer him up, and Anthony did his best to pretend, but even several episodes of Oz didn't manage to make him crack a smile.

He sat on the couch and stared at the screen in a fog before wandering over to his bedroom in a funk, sliding into the bed he should be sharing with Renee, abandoning his nightly routines, deciding not to brush his teeth just like he decided not to visit the specialist despite incessant begging from the most important person in his life.

Anthony was still lying in that bed as the sun rose, with half of him wanting to do better — jump up and wrestle this new day to the ground — while the other half wanted to stay buried under the covers for another week or so.

But then a scent struck his nostrils, and he heard the cooking sounds in the kitchen.

He jumped out of bed and rushed toward the door without even stopping to use the restroom, either forgetting that Michael was staying with them or disregarding it in light of the fantasy that it might be Renee downstairs, cooking him a big breakfast to go with a French press full of coffee.

But it was Michael, not Renee, standing over a skillet of eggs. He turned from the stove and grinned at Anthony. "What up, cuz? I cook breakfast, and that's the look you give me?"

"Sorry. I thought you might be Renee."

"Right ..." Michael turned back to his eggs. "Because that's how this works."

"What are you making?" Anthony asked, coming over to stand beside the stove.

"Just finishing the eggs to go with the bacon. Pancakes have been done for a while."

"Seriously?" Anthony looked over at the counter and saw that his cousin hadn't been kidding. "What's the occasion?"

"No occasion." Michael shrugged. "Unless you count your life sucking. In that case, your life would be the occasion."

"Screw you," Anthony said, shoving a piece of bacon into his mouth, then grabbing another one before he finished swallowing.

"Go ahead. Eat up. We have a big day."

"Whtrewdng?" *What are we doing?*

"I've told all our neighbors that the fish fry is off—"

"*My* neighbors."

"—and you don't have a job. Your radiation starts tomorrow, so I figure that now is the time to buck up and do something that we always used to do together."

"Pull leeches off of your ass?"

"Nope." Michael shook his head, laughing. "But that only happened *one* time. I said something we *always* used to do together."

148

"What, then?"

"You'll see." He turned off the skillet, added eggs to the plate of bacon, and handed the whole thing to Anthony. "Here."

"You're not eating?"

"I already ate a bowl of oatmeal. I ain't looking to get fat."

"What makes you think I am?" Anthony grabbed another piece of bacon, hurrying into the living room for his pancakes.

"I'm not saying you are, but you could use the weight—"

"Ntlkitsmusl." *Not like it's muscle.*

"—and judging by last night, it seemed like a safe bet that this morning you'd be into eating your feelings."

"*Illeeturflngs.*" *I'll eat your feelings.*

Michael laughed but didn't reply, then sat across from Anthony and let him chew in silence, the pair of them staring out the window at a neighborhood withering on its vine.

"So when do I get to know what we're doing today?" Anthony asked.

"As soon as you can guess." Michael waved him toward the door.

"Does it look like I'm ready to go anywhere? Shit, at least let me put on some clothes and go to the bathroom."

"Maybe you should do it the other way around."

Anthony ignored him, quickly getting ready, then meeting Michael outside. He gestured Anthony into his Jeep, but they didn't get far, stopping at The Canopy without explanation.

"I'll be right back," Michael said.

"Where are you going?"

"To pick up something from Joy." Then he slammed the door with no further explanation.

Anthony shook his head, alone in the Jeep. Michael returned a few minutes later, holding a plastic container filled with something in his lap.

"What is that?" Anthony asked.

"You ain't never seen a Tupperware before?" Michael replied as if that were answer enough.

"Joy Jones is making you lunch?"

"I'd like to see you eat what's in here," Michael said.

Anthony shook his head again, knowing better than to ask anything else.

So he drove in silence, thinking about how he could apologize to Renee and prove that he meant it, starting with finding the dog she adored so much. Even after ruminating on the many escalating ways of saying *sorry*, he still had no idea where they were going and didn't want to ask, sure he'd get it eventually like Michael obviously wanted him to.

Anthony kept following directions, finally figuring it out five or so miles shy of their destination. "We're going fishing, aren't we?"

"That we are." Michael slapped his knee.

Directions were no longer necessary. Anthony had never driven outside the city to the river by the woods, but he knew where it was. Which meant that he knew what was in the Tupperware. Not lunch, but bait. Chicken guts specifically, and probably some string.

The cousins were going fishing for crawfish, just like they did when they were kids.

Anthony parked, and they walked toward the water. He felt surprisingly — almost shockingly — content. The nostalgia was there, but the fishing felt different. They were no longer boys and not nearly as boisterous.

Especially not today.

Michael sat quietly while Anthony reflected on his choices.

This wasn't just a right-now problem. It was an always problem, which meant it was something he needed to fix if he expected to get the life with Renee he'd been longing for.

More than a problem, this was a pattern. One he'd leveled on her over and over. Every time there had been something serious looming ahead (like their move to Atlanta, or the decision to get his last job, or their upcoming flight from the neighborhood), he'd find a way to distract himself by diving into some elaborate project.

While holding a string full of chicken guts and dangling his feet in the water, Anthony realized that although he'd been pulling similar crap all of his life, it mattered more than ever because now he was doing it to Renee. Instead of acting like the partner she deserved, he'd been a hurdle impeding their growth.

Anthony had abandoned her to do all the adulting by herself, leaving his wife with the difficult decisions and expecting her to drag him along.

She deserved better, and he knew it. The string of chicken guts was a fair representation of his feelings. He needed some way to show Renee how much he appreciated her and all of the sacrifices she had made by being the one in their relationship who was accountable to the reality of their situation instead of the rose-tinted fiction he usually (always) wanted to see.

"Do you think there's any hope of me winning Renee back?"

"Like she's a carnival prize?" Michael laughed. "Win the ringtoss and get another shot at—"

"You know what I mean, smartass."

"Better a smartass than a dumbass." Michael shrugged but didn't say anything else.

"That's all I get? You're really not gonna answer me?"

"Why did it take you so damn long to go to the doctor?" Michael asked, his tone suddenly sober. "Renee wasn't nagging you out of nowhere. She was asking you to get checked out because of your headaches. Shit, man, half the time I looked over, I saw you squeezing your nose like a zit."

"Because …" Anthony sighed before telling the truth. "If I knew if something was wrong, that would change everything."

"Life is about change, man."

"But so much of my life was already changing … If I didn't go to the doctor, I wouldn't have to face that change," Anthony admitted.

"You think that's how a real man handles things?"

"You seriously think gender has anything to do with it?"

"You know what I mean, man."

Anthony did, but still, he didn't reply.

"Have I ever told you why I've always traveled so much instead of living life just one way?"

"No." Anthony shook his head.

"I can't stay in one place too long for one simple reason: the more you see in life, the better you get to know yourself. And that's the key to a good life, cuz. Knowing who you are means knowing who you can be."

"You sound like a fortune cookie."

But Anthony didn't really mean that, and Michael knew it. "Who you are is the sum total of all the different moments in your life that truly mattered."

"What are you actually trying to say right now?" Anthony asked.

"That we brought something small but special to your neighbors. Whether or not we were able to save the neighborhood is irrelevant. We shared a tradition and sharing that tradition helped to keep it alive. You get what I'm saying, man?" Michael looked over at Anthony, then answered himself. "The differences and changes are what help give meaning to our lives."

But Anthony still had a question in his eyes, so Michael continued.

"Grandmoh used to say that we could never wish change away. Nothing can last forever, and even if it could, would we really want it to?" Michael shook his head, again answering his own question ahead of Anthony. "Of course not. Because then life would be boring. You won't always be in the places you love most, but you can be responsible for creating all of those feelings of family and home wherever you go."

"And that's what you do when you travel?" Anthony asked.

"That's not just what I do when I travel, man. It's *why* I travel in the first place."

Then Michael fell silent, either because he wanted Anthony to steep in his words or because he was truly finished with what he wanted to say. Mission accomplished either way. Now Anthony couldn't stop considering the wisdom of his cousin's words.

The conversation itself was surprising, forcing Anthony to look at Michael in a way he never had before. He'd always been his favorite cousin, but Anthony had also seen Michael as a party guy who could never settle down. But that wasn't true at all: a life full of travel and the experience that came with it had given his cousin a depth that Anthony could only now acknowledge.

After a while, the sun and sparkle of the water did their

work in calming Anthony down and ushering him into the moment. He felt like that little boy again, thrilling at the crawdads nipping at his line. Michael was like a smaller version of his father, Jamal. The afternoon felt full of all the joy and peace of those long-remembered Louisiana days.

The cousins competed to see who could pull the most (and biggest) crayfish from the little river but lost count as their cooler filled.

Considering all the things going wrong in his life, Anthony felt surprisingly spry on their drive home. It was a good day, filled with things he needed to hear, even if he didn't want to.

He swung onto Edgewood as the sun was saying good-bye, exhausted but at peace, a cooler full of crawdads in back, ready to boil.

"That was a great day, cuz," Anthony said. "Thank you ... I think I really needed that."

"I *know* you really needed that. But you're welcome, man."

Then Michael went to the back for the crawdads while Anthony went to unlock the door.

He made it halfway before turning toward the sound of barking behind him and saw Rob and Riley running toward him, holding Fry Guy by the collar.

"You found him!" Anthony shouted in delighted surprise.

"It took almost the whole day," Riley reported, "but we took a bunch of neighbors looking, and we finally found him."

"Ezekiel almost shot us," Rob said.

"Oh my God." Riley rolled her eyes. "Ezekiel did not almost shoot us. He just *threatened* to shoot us if we didn't get off his lawn."

"That was until he realized it was us, and then he jumped the fence on the abandoned house next door, and we saw Fry Guy pawing at the back door."

Anthony captured both his neighbors in a hug that surprised them. His gratitude for the people showing up in his life was palpable.

That night Anthony curled up in bed while Fry Guy slept on Renee's side. He fell asleep with a smile, dreaming of tomorrow when he would deliver the dog to Renee.

Chapter Twenty-Three

ANTHONY SLEPT LIKE A BABY.

Or, since plenty of babies screamed through the night so far as he knew, Anthony actually slept like a man who might finally be edging the outskirts of peace with himself. Yes, he had made a disaster of things, but now he was at the doctor's office, waiting his turn to make everything right.

Fry Guy was with the bros. They promised to feed and play with him until Anthony got back home, needing the little puppy to love him.

It was a big day. His first radiation appointment. If not for all that time spent connecting with his cousin, Anthony wouldn't be anywhere near ready for this. But now, he was bolstered, if not buoyed. Of course, things would be okay. They always were. Michael was wiser than Anthony had given him credit for. Maybe he should start backpacking all over creation, too.

Except that Anthony had the rest of his life to do that, and right now, he needed to reconnect with Renee, apologize with Fry Guy, and all his sincerity. Make her feel seen and heard. Acknowledge her feelings, and promise to do better now that he knew better.

But first, he had to get through the next few hours. Anthony was scared in a way that he'd never been frightened before. It was brutal how deep the terror kept sinking, forcing him to stare death in the eye decades earlier than he'd ever allowed himself to imagine.

Unfortunately, being ready to face reality didn't dilute the shock.

Two patients were waiting in the room besides Anthony. He'd made himself at home in the corner, approximately equidistant from the others. Michael had promised to meet him there, but so far, his cousin hadn't appeared.

The door swung open, but instead of Michael, it was a small girl with bright blue hair holding a trio of balloons. She took a single step and then paused in the doorway, looking around the room before her eyes settled on Anthony.

She gave him a tiny smile, then timidly shuffled over to the seat right across from him. Dad squeezed her shoulder and kept walking toward the receptionist to check them in.

"I like your hair," she said.

"Thank you." Anthony found himself touching his locs without meaning to.

"I think it's super cool." Another smile, this one wider.

"I think your hair is cool, too. I love the color blue. You must have cool parents to let you dye it like that."

"It's not real," she admitted with a whisper, followed by a gentle lifting of her hair to show him her bald head underneath. "It's a wig. I started to lose my hair last month."

"Oh." He felt slapped. Tried to find a smile. Made it halfway there. "It sure looks like the real thing!"

"Everyone says that."

He hoped the shock wasn't too apparent on his face. A little girl with a bunch of balloons coming in with her father. Anthony had assumed she was there to visit a relative going through chemo ... not that the poor girl would be going through the treatment herself.

He hadn't even thought about losing his locs until that moment, though, of course, it was obvious. But after even just a few words with this little girl, Anthony no longer cared. She was braver than he was. Losing his hair was the last thing he should be worrying about.

"My name's Anthony." He offered his hand.

"I'm Macy. I can't tell you my last name because you're a stranger."

"That's smart." He nodded. "I promise not to ask your middle name either."

Macy smiled. "Was that a joke?"

"My wife would say that it wasn't."

She scrunched her nose. "Was that another joke?"

"Is this your first time?"

Macy shook her head. "It's my third week." She looked up at her balloons. "My dad buys them every time."

"They are very nice balloons." Anthony nodded again. They were, though all three looked bootleg. One had a kind of Care Bear, but instead of having a rainbow on its chest, the wannabe was wearing the love on its shirt. A second balloon boasted some kind of bastardized Pokémon, and the third featured a cowboy riding his unicorn — Anthony wasn't sure what that was supposed to be.

Macy shrugged, leaned a little closer, and whispered, "I don't really like balloons."

Anthony whispered back. "Why don't you like balloons?"

"They're bad for the environment." Still a secret, but delivered with sorrow.

"Then why do you get them?" Anthony whispered back, but he already kind of knew.

"It makes my dad feel better." She shrugged. "It was fine the first week, but then the next week, I got two balloons. And today, I got three. What about next week and the week after that?" Macy shook her head. "I have to find a way to tell him."

"You're a smart girl," Anthony started.

But then Macy said, "Can't I just be smart?"

"Of course." He smiled, loving this child as he corrected himself. "You're obviously smart, for a lot of reasons. And I think it's great you care so much about the environment. And about your father's feelings. You just need to tell him the truth. You'll know the right words at the right time. Just don't be afraid to have the hard conversation."

"You're smart too," said the girl with an affirmative nod.

"Macy Daniels!" called a woman in cat-printed scrubs, holding a clipboard and standing in front of an open door.

Macy stood from her seat with a shrug. "I guess you know my last name now."

"Then I guess that means we're not strangers."

Another strong nod. "It was nice to meet you, Anthony. Good luck in there. I hope you get to keep all your hair."

"Me too."

"Come on, Macy." Dad waved her forward and smiled at Anthony.

He was alone and thinking for another few minutes, mostly about making up with Renee, then one day having a baby and watching it grow into a little girl, hopefully, smart like Macy—

The door swung open, and again it wasn't Michael, but this time the person in the doorway stole all of Anthony's breath.

He leapt up from his seat.

"Sit down," Renee said, walking toward him, clutching a brown paper bag.

He collapsed back in his seat. She took the one next to him, then pulled him against her. He cried as she hugged him.

"How did you know where I was?" he finally asked.

"Michael called me."

"Of course he did." Anthony wiped at his eyes. "I'm so sorry that I didn't get checked earlier—"

"It's fine, Anthony." She gave him a reassuring smile. "I promise." She moved the bag into the crook of her arm and placed a hand over his. "I'm just happy that we're dealing with it now."

"Me too." He put his hand over hers. "But it's still important that I tell you I was wrong for sticking my head in the sand, just like you said I was. You deserve a man who sees you and hears you, not just says the words but does the deeds. I promise I'm that man, Renee."

"I know you are." A tear slid down her cheek. "And there's nothing we can't face together."

Anthony knew that to be true, but his next confession terrified him. "I got fired."

Renee's face went still for only a moment. "Scott Hodson's a real prick."

"That he is." Anthony laughed and pulled his wife into another hug. He nodded toward the bag. "What's in there?"

Renee smiled as she opened it, then stuffed her hand inside and pulled out a baseball cap.

Anthony laughed as she handed it to him, already

understanding exactly what this was. He looked down at the hat, pretending to study the Saints logo to keep himself from meeting her eyes and crying again.

"If you can't still be the locs guy, then maybe you can become the hat guy."

It hurt how well she knew him.

Anthony looked up, met her eyes, and started crying anyway.

Chapter Twenty-Four

ANTHONY'S first time at chemo was mercifully over.

He wanted to get all the cancer stuff out of his head so he could focus on the reunion with Renee. But perhaps having to take separate cars was a blessing. It gave him a chance to process everything that happened and all that he'd learned about what was going to happen before they got home. Then Anthony could focus on her.

He was prepared for the side effects. Doctor Aubrey had told him to expect nausea, vomiting, and fatigue, plus plenty of reminders that eating well and regular exercise could help to curb the worst of it. He knew the IV was coming because his chemo was intravenous.

They took his blood, and he met with his oncologist to check his overall health and the blood test results. He met the nurse and caregiving staff. He had his blood pressure, pulse, and temperature taken. He stood on the scale and got reminded of his height. Then, finally, he got a needle in his arm.

But at least he had Renee, and what a world of difference that made.

She pulled up at the house a few seconds before him, but Anthony was reasonably sure that he spotted Kevin waiting on their front stoop first.

Kevin came running over to the Wrangler and was already there before Anthony could open the door. He was jumping up and down like a kid, barely able to contain himself.

"When's the last time you went to the bathroom?" Anthony asked.

"We went viral!" Kevin exclaimed.

"You and your pee?"

"DUDE, THIS IS SERIOUS!"

"What's serious?" Renee asked as she closed her car door.

"Yeah, whatcha talkin' 'bout, Willis?" Anthony said.

"PERRY ABRAHAM—"

"But not so loud," Renee told him, patting the air in front of her.

Kevin started over, slightly calmer. "Perry Abraham retweeted your post."

"No shit ..." Anthony's hand was over his mouth.

"What post?" Renee looked from Kevin to Anthony.

"He wrote a post about the fish fry: *Life's a Fish and Then You Fry.* Like I said, it went viral after Perry Abraham retweeted it."

"No shit ..." echoed Renee.

Perry Abraham was a big deal everywhere, but here in Atlanta, Anthony wouldn't have been surprised to see statues of the guy. People loved Abraham: his movies, his politics, his hair, and his scarves. The man was funny and loyal, and generous. People naturally wanted to like the same things that he liked. A simple retweet from Perry Abraham felt more like an anointment.

"I can't believe it …" Anthony was shaking his head. "How do you think he found it?"

"It was probably right there in his inbox after I sent it to him."

Anthony didn't know what to say. He still couldn't believe it. After trying for words and failing, he gave up and pulled his buddy into a bear hug. Kevin didn't know where he'd been or why and didn't really know much about what was happening between him and Renee, yet here he was with a lifeline.

It wasn't that he still wanted to hold the fish fry, the idea of *bringing a little Louisiana into your life* was apparently catching on.

"Impressive," Renee said after her man had failed to find the words.

"Seriously," Anthony echoed.

Kevin shrugged. "I knew Abraham likes to have fun and loves a small-town hero story. He's also from Louisiana, so sending it his way seemed like a no-brainer."

"I would normally love to agree with anything having to do with your lack of brains, but this was damned smart. Thank you."

"YO!" Michael called, running across the street with Rob by his side.

"Perry Abraham—" Anthony started.

"Retweeted your post, and now everyone thinks you're awesome?" Rob finished.

"You think Kevin just stood here and waited without coming over to brag about how awesome he is?" Michael asked.

"I wasn't bragging about—"

"He's just kidding," Anthony explained. "But there's a small problem. The fish fry is off."

"I hear you, man, but it can't be." Michael took the

ball. "Your boy Rob built a little website for the event like—"

"More like a mini-site," Rob interjected.

"—a week ago, *just in case*."

"It wasn't hard." Rob shrugged. "Because, WordPress."

"Why would you build a website for a one-time fish fry?" Renee asked.

"Mini-site," Rob corrected.

"*Just in case,*" Michael explained again.

"Just in case, what?" Renee creased her face in curious expectation.

Rob tried to help. "Just in case we needed it."

But he didn't.

"Needed it for—" Renee started.

"He can go all day," Michael said, cutting her off. "Point is, we've had over a thousand hits, and they're still coming fast, so there's no stopping this rolling ball now."

"The fry is the day after tomorrow, and it's happening whether you want it or not," Rob told Anthony.

"Thank you for adding nothing to the conversation." Michael slapped Rob on the shoulder.

Anthony looked at Renee, and they traded their pain in a gaze.

Then he said, "I really, really appreciate everything you all have done for the fish fry, but there's no real point to it anymore. Darius has already sold ... there isn't really a neighborhood to save ... not anymore."

"That's true." Renee nodded. "But I bet there are a hell of a lot of ATLiens who could use a little Louisiana in their lives."

"True that," Rob said.

"Stop watching *The Wire*," Michael told him.

"Are we really having a fish fry?" The width of Anthony's grin shouldn't have been possible, considering he'd started the day with his first round of chemo.

"We are *definitely* having a fish fry." Renee came up beside Anthony and grabbed his hand. Then she squeezed it tightly as she kissed him.

"So, where were you guys?" Kevin asked.

Anthony's answer was killed by a bark as Fry Guy ran right up to Renee, pursued by two of the bros.

"There you are!" She sat down right in the street to hug her puppy, and Anthony thought that it was worth every ounce of chemo to see his wife so happy.

"Hello over dere!"

Everyone turned toward the shout as Darius wheeled his way up the sidewalk. He looked fierce yet gentle, shoving his arms down to push the wheels while making it seem like he was gliding just a breeze above the concrete.

Darius stopped in front of the group but turned his gaze on Anthony. "I just wanted to thank you. For everything you've been doing to try and save the neighborhood. I could never properly tell you what it means to me, but I could sure as hell come over here and give you a proper *good job* myself."

He nodded at Anthony, and it felt like a second *good job*.

"Joy can always keep a secret exactly as long as she wants to, so it's no surprise that she finally saw fit to tell me what you all have been doing. Especially you." Another nod at Anthony. "If this was just a few years ago, I'd still be waving the flag right alongside you. But I'm already old, and it feels like I'm getting older a lot faster than I used to."

Darius shrugged. "I decided to go ahead and sell. I'm ready for this. Maybe even excited. No more trying to open jars. Life is supposed to keep changing, but me and mine have been in the same place for a while now. I'm excited to see what happens next."

"I'm excited, too." Anthony offered his hand.

Darius shook it with gusto. "Sorry, we didn't to get to know one another better sooner."

"We're having a fish fry in two days. Come by, and we can get to know each other better then."

"I almost like that ..." Darius sounded like he might have a serious objection.

"What *don't* you like about it?" Anthony asked.

"Seems that a man such as myself might know a thing or two about holding a fish fry and that a man such as myself might also like to lend his know-how to the cause."

"I'd be delighted," Anthony said, extending his hand again.

"Then it's a deal," Darius replied, shaking it.

Chapter Twenty-Five

THE ENTIRE NEXT day was a blur of preparation.

The cul-de-sac got going early. Anthony was ready before he went to sleep the night before, waking up a half-hour ahead of his alarm only to find that Renee had already beaten him. The aroma met him as he opened his eyes. A few minutes later, he met her in the kitchen with a kiss that tasted even better than the French press full of Kenyan.

"Want to guess where Michael is right now?" Renee asked with a smile.

"Looking for a pair of shoes that could add another inch to his height?"

She laughed, but it sounded to Anthony like a courtesy. "He's at The Canopy. Guess what he's doing there ..."

Anthony took a sip of his coffee while waiting to see if there was more to that story.

"You know it would be much more efficient if you were to just tell me," he said when there wasn't.

"He's talking to Manny from 187. According to Darius, some of the gang actually do security for a living. He

168

thinks he can talk them into covering security in exchange for good food and some good times."

Anthony laughed at his cousin's audacity. "Should I call and wish him luck with that?"

But the joke was on Anthony; he wasn't even finished with his coffee before Michael came into the house, loudly announcing his victory. "Who's the best-looking guy on this street *and* the one who landed top-flight security for free?"

"It's not free if we're feeding them," Anthony said.

Michael rolled his eyes. "Plus the cost of hearing your bullshit."

The day rolled forward like it was on rails. Kevin went to the print shop and picked up the T-shirts, with boxes split down the middle between the ones with *Atlanta Fish Fry* and a fleur-de-lis on the back and *Life's a Fish and Then You Fry,* both shirts in green and purple. The tees were for the neighborhood, giving the "staff" a way to patrol and monitor the event.

Joy Jones wrangled the bros into an assembly line in her kitchen, using them to mix, sift, arrange, and otherwise aid her in making and baking an impressive array of desserts and side dishes. She also claimed to have dragged her son into the swing of things, though it seemed to Anthony that Keith didn't need the prompting. He appeared perfectly happy, if not downright overjoyed, to use his company — music promoters, or so it turned out — to set up a full stage right in the wide ring of the cul-de-sac.

The Pattersons were working as a father and son team like they might have been back in their good old days, kneeling in the grass, making signs for the fish fry's various booths, including but not limited to face painting, beads, Mardi Gras wear, and candle making — Anthony didn't want to ask about that last one. Not only had they cleared all of Wendall's Bible quotes to make room for the new messaging, they even made a sign for Junkman to sell his wares. The sign read *JUNK YOU NEED NOW!*, which Anthony considered a rather effective bit of copywriting. Ezekiel was a natural.

Wherever Anthony looked, he saw hard work and smiles. A community coming together. Neighbors turning into friends thanks to the alchemy of intention and attention met by a need to have fun. Laughter was everywhere. Though the music wasn't yet blasting, the party had already started.

Riley and Rob were sourcing grills and fryers from all over the city to accommodate the massive amount of fish Kevin had convinced the market to donate in exchange for sponsorship. Fish market signs were put up in windows and hammered into front lawns.

Renee was at home, listening to Beyoncé at full blast while making an ocean of Jell-O shots. Green and purple, arranged like bouquets at a wedding throughout the room. She was moving to the music, wiggling her rear without any idea that Anthony was admiring the view, ruminating on how lucky he was to still have the one thing he should never have allowed himself to risk losing in the first place.

She turned around, saw him watching, and smiled back with both her mouth and her eyes, still sashaying to the beat, even fiercer now that she knew her man was watching.

He could have stood there all day, but Anthony had things to do.

Like cleaning the house, top to bottom.

Not an easy task. He was struggling to do anything at all in the wake of his first chemo appointment. Just walking around to check in on everyone was exhausting enough.

But he was determined to do his share, regardless of how he felt. The entire neighborhood was working together like ingredients in a big pot of gumbo, coalescing to transform individual components into a complex yet singular taste. So he left with a kiss, then got right to his cleaning.

Anthony was fine for the first hour and glad that the bathroom door was closed when he finally lost it — *it* being what felt like several gallons of vomit. But at least the music was loud, and he'd lost his cookies inside a freshly scrubbed toilet.

He was still on the floor when the noise kept getting louder and louder outside until it was finally too much of a cacophony to ignore.

He slowly stood and made his way to the window.

The stage was almost set, with Keith smiling wide and shouting directions. Clusters of neighbors peppered the cul-de-sac, only about half of whom Anthony recognized. He saw a surprising number of dogs, three of which were wearing costumes for some reason.

He was still smiling at the window when a truck from Back to the Bayou pulled onto Edgewood with a trio of light honks. It stopped at the end of the street, then a round woman and a wizened man from the Louisiana-themed store each got out from their side of the vehicle, meeting in the rear to raise the back hatch.

The smell of meat hit Anthony like a slap. He told himself that the scent was delicious and not making him nauseous. He ignored the roll in his stomach while watching the workers unload beads, decorations, and five boxes labeled *Tony Chachere's Fish Fry Seasoning*.

Renee's music was gone from the kitchen, but the house was even louder than before, thanks to the constant foot traffic coming in and out of the house from well-wishers and workers alike.

He went back to work, scrubbing the toilet again and turning the glass into an ad for Windex. He caught his breath, then got back to work on the baseboards. But once on his knees, he heard a tremendous clatter coming from outside. Not like the truck from Back to the Bayou, but maybe ten of them.

He got back up and looked out the window, only then remembering that Michael had left on a final mission. Now he was back with a truck, hauling a trailer full of porta-potties.

Anthony laughed and dropped his cleaning rags. Now he could give Renee the biggest gift of all: locking up the house and keeping the party entirely on the street.

He couldn't believe they were really having a fish fry tomorrow. The event truly brought a community together. They had done this. They were ready to go. They still had to set everything up on the street, but that would have to wait until morning.

He should probably go out there. Was it time for dinner?

Anthony had lost track of time, and he wasn't wearing a watch. But—

The door opened and stole his chance to decide. Renee looked down at her man sprawled in front of the baseboards. Then she started laughing.

"What do you think you're doing?"

"I'm cleaning the bathroom."

"And it looks amazing. Great job. But the baseboards? I thought no one ever noticed the baseboards?"

A wink, a wiggling of his eyebrows, and, "The women will notice."

"Nobody will notice." She laughed again. "They aren't even coming in here."

"You'll notice."

Another laugh, then she got down beside him. They leaned their heads against each other, sharing a long and silent moment before Anthony sighed and pulled away to take her hands.

"I could never have done this without you," he said.

She smiled and waited, knowing there was more.

"I couldn't have done it without everyone, of course. But you're the most important person in the world to me. And I'm sorry for all the times I've failed to prove it."

"Stop it, Anthony." She kissed him, then stood and held out her hand. "There's something we need to do."

He took her hand and stood. "What is it?"

"You know," she said as they stared into the mirror together.

Then she quietly and carefully sheared his locs.

They looked at his bald head together, then she placed the Saints cap like a crown on his head and said, "You've never looked better."

Chapter Twenty-Six

ANTHONY WOKE up from what might have been the deepest sleep of his life.

Renee was snuggled up next to him, running a hand over his shiny and freshly shaved head. Fry Guy was at the foot of their bed between them. They had been lying against each other long enough that their inhales and exhales were in perfect time.

Excitement for the day was like a live wire snaking its way across the bed. Yet neither spoke of it, awake but basking in silence, wanting to linger rather than hurry through their morning as a prelude to an unforgettable day.

But their solitude was gone for good when they bolted up in bed together.

"NO!" Anthony cried out, his feet already touching the floor.

Renee followed and met him at the window.

There wasn't a warning drizzle; the sky simply opened to drop a monsoon of rain. Buckets were falling, splashing on the roofs of houses and cars, drowning the street, and dragging their day into the gutter.

"Maybe it'll stop …"

Though, of course, Renee knew that rain like this didn't just stop. If anything, the downpour was only now getting started. But she didn't know that the weather insurance had never been purchased.

By the time they threw on some clothes and managed to get outside with a pair of umbrellas, it seemed like half of the neighborhood had already beat them. It was hard to see who was who through the wall of umbrellas, coming in a rainbow of colors and a medley of sizes.

"There's no coming back from this, is there?" Riley asked.

"It would have to stop raining like *right now*," Rob replied, casting a dubious gaze to the sky.

The crowd began to mutter among itself.

Anthony heard the door open behind him, then turned to see Michael descending the stoop, his jaw set and his eyes full of sorrow, shoulders looking like an invisible bag of flour was strapped to each of them, his gait crooked with disappointment.

"You gotta be shitting me," he muttered.

"I shit you not." Anthony ran a hand across his gleaming head. Then, hard as it was, he ripped off the Band-Aid. "I didn't get weather insurance."

Renee chewed on her bottom lip, cycling through a list of possible responses before settling on a sigh as she took him by the hand.

"At least it's not like we still need to save the neighborhood," Anthony said.

"But we'll lose a lot of money if the fish fry doesn't happen," Renee replied. "And the neighborhood that we no longer have to save will start reeking if we don't cook all of that fish.

The crowd started gathering around them, wanting to join the conversation.

"We had a new goal," Jonah announced.

"We wanted to help Anthony with his cancer payments," said Carter.

Then Josh: "He's the one who started all of this, and he needs the help, so we all sorta figured that would be the best way to spend any money we made from the fish fry."

Anthony was out of a job and insurance at the worst possible moment, but that didn't make him a charity case. He just wasn't wired to accept something for nothing.

He smiled at the crowd. "I would have had to kindly refuse the offer, but I sure do appreciate it." Another smile. "I'm okay, I promise. We'll figure out a way to make it work. The good and the bad come together, and right now, the good in my life *far* outweighs the bad."

The patter of drops upon umbrellas was percussion for this memory. The rain had lightened ever so slightly, but the sky was still a bruise. And yet the moment was beautiful, with no one in any hurry to leave.

"What would we have done with the money if the fry had gone on and Anthony refused to take it?" Keith asked the crowd.

"Fund a new church," Wendall suggested.

"Buy all of the Junkman's junk and clean up his yard," offered Joy Jones.

"I know exactly where I'd want to send that money." Anthony imagined Macy holding her three mylar balloons. He pictured her with five, then nine, and then … none.

Because just like him, Macy was going to be okay.

After much discussion, the group determined that Anthony's suggestion was best. They would have donated their theoretical funds to an organization aiding low-income patients with help paying their medical bills.

He changed the subject. "Well, our house is clean. Anyone want to join us inside for some coffee?"

"We have plenty of Kenyan," Renee added with warmth and a smile.

Everyone followed them inside, congregating in the living and dining rooms, with some spillover into the kitchen. Anthony didn't mind the crowd in his space, and somehow Renee seemed to mind it even less, still smiling as she prepared the coffee.

"So, let's take a vote." Michael raised his right hand. "Who thinks Anthony here is a dumbass for not getting weather insurance?" He shook his head. "Never mind. Strike that. Not fair. I think we can all agree he was being a dumbass, and it isn't cool for us to all pile on him like that, especially after he just got cancer—"

"Turns out I've had it for a while. I just found out," Anthony interrupted.

"He's always ruining my jokes," Michael complained.

"I think you do that fine yourself."

"Anyway," Michael turned back to the crowd, "since we can all agree that he's a dumbass, let's work on a spectrum. If you think he's a ten when it comes to being a dumbass for not getting insurance, raise your hand."

No one raised their hand.

"They're just being nice to you," Michael explained.

"Why don't you try being nice to him!" Renee snapped.

Anthony addressed the crowd. "I'm sorry that I didn't get weather insurance, but I did use the money to buy a lot of food and the best band known to humanity, all of which we can still enjoy … I hope. Plus, we'll have some amazing fireworks for later."

"When?" Renee asked.

"The next time it's clear outside!"

She rolled her eyes, then kissed him on the cheek.

Riley and Rob joined Renee in the kitchen, starting a second pot of coffee to go with the press, and getting a batch of hot chocolate going as well.

Once the beverages were ready, the neighbors gathered for stories, starting with Miss Adelaide telling them all about her yesteryear and the life she almost had in South America, back when she was in love with an Argentinian teacher. They had plans to marry, but her aging mother had a heart attack, so Miss Adelaide (then named Missy, hilariously enough) was forced to cancel her plans and come home to be her mother's caretaker.

"You know," Miss Adelaide said at the end of her story, "I used to think that all my dreams died along with my mother and that she kind of talked them away even before she was gone, whether she meant to or not. But now I know better." She nodded to herself. "Now I realize I wasn't stopped by my mother's illness so much as fear of change." She nodded again. "Fear of the unknown."

Miss Adelaide fell quiet, and the room exhaled with her.

Wendall broke the silence as he gestured out the window. "Come look ... it's a miracle."

Wendall was right: there was indeed a miracle outside.

Everyone clustered around the window, staring through the glass at an eager sun spilling light from the freshly cleared skies down onto the still-soaking streets.

Anthony looked around the room, feeling hope from his neighbors like a backbeat. He ran an absentminded hand across his gleaming dome — a new and improved unconscious habit, much better than the pinching inspired by his migraines — then raised his arms and shouted, "If you're ready, scream from the top of your lungs. LIFE'S A FISH AND THEN YOU FRRRYYYYYYY!"

After everyone repeated the chant from the top of their lungs, the room erupted in an uproarious cheer, then scrambled into motion without Anthony or Renee, or anyone else having to issue a single direction.

The neighborhood went to work, laughing through the setup. The bros ran up and down the street, hanging fleur-de-lis on every naked surface. Renee and Riley ran to drag the knick-knack booths out of their garages and onto the street. At the same time, Anthony, Michael, Rob, Kevin, and Keith got an army of grills like soldiers awaiting orders in an assembly of yards, removing sections of fence so they could all cook together.

Throughout it all, Anthony felt like he was two-thirds emotion, wanting to cry at half of all he saw. Like the neighborhood working as a single unit; the steady chorus of genuine laughter; Renee bustling around the street with a smile while Fry Guy kept pace at her heels, unwilling to abandon his new best friend for even a moment.

They fired up the grills and fryers as Ezekiel loaded tables with boxes of Jell-O shots.

Anthony glanced at his watch. In a half-hour or so, their guests would be arriving. Or so he thought.

Looking up, he saw that the rain hadn't deterred their guests in the least. Cars were already turning onto the cul-de-sac early.

And there were a lot of them.

Chapter Twenty-Seven

THE FINAL FISH fry was a flurry of controlled chaos.

The party was *everywhere*. Of course, it covered every part of the street, but the festivities also spread across nearly every lawn — including the patches of wheat-colored grass fronting the foreclosures — and onto porches and stoops. Laughter was almost operatic, ringing through the neighborhood and bringing people from nearby streets over as much as the music from Down in the Treme belting it out onstage.

Residents of the cul-de-sac were wearing their special shirts, helping direct the crowd, and manage the fun. The street was still a bit wet, and the whole shebang a little messier than it would have been otherwise, but that only added to the festive atmosphere.

Anthony looked around at all the memories occurring in real-time.

A congregation of kids with painted faces were running in circles, playing with wild abandon, weaving in and out of each other while whooping and hollering between visits to the tables covered with food.

There were untold heaps of fish, but Anthony had no doubt it would all be gone before sundown. Jovial arguments occasionally erupted as guests and neighbors argued over which seasoning deserved the crown: Tony Chachere's or Lawry's. There were a few Lawry's supporters in the crowd, but each time the controversy arose, they were hilariously shouted right down.

A Lawry's lover might say, "Tony Chachere's is too damn salty! Sure, I like a little shake in my dish, but Chachere's is two-thirds salt to one-third spice."

To which a Tony Chachere's supporter would reply, "The only thing Chachere ain't great on is ice cream."

Tables that weren't filled with food were packed with cards, and the small crowds of people throwing them down. The air was thick with horn-infused music, blasting through the neighborhood with such boot-stomping ferocity Anthony imagined cartoon notes bouncing just under the clouds. Down in the Treme was worth every dollar.

"You do realize that this is because of the article you wrote, right?" Kevin reminded him.

Modesty had Anthony shaking his head. "Nothing attracts a crowd like a crowd."

"Sure. But you still started it." Kevin pointed to the nearest table of food. "You wrote about taking a little Louisiana with you wherever you go, and just look at how people responded."

Anthony followed Kevin's finger and saw how right he was.

The table was a trip to Louisiana thanks to all the sides, not just from Back to the Bayou. Guests and neighbors alike had helped fill the table with gumbo, shrimp etouffee, crawfish monicas, muffulettas, po-boys, boudin, fried green tomatoes, plus an absolute bounty of rice and beans.

But the day wasn't without its problems. The loud girl with the louder hair from the second fry had returned, this time with a pair of even rowdier companions. She seemed as addicted to hair dye as she was to attention — last time, it was bright pink and this time an iridescent yellow — and had apparently brought the men to fight over her. One was a hulk and the other a beanpole, but the twig of a man looked like he'd been born with a temper that had only been boiling since. Hulk looked almost gentle, though still ready to start throwing blows. He was wearing a shirt that somehow managed to make Anthony feel uncomfortable. It read, *Mass is a Seance.* Yellow Hair stood two feet away as they stared each other down, both with clenched fists and ready to use them.

But that's what security was for. Anthony didn't have to say anything. Or even point. Manny from 187 was already on it.

Manny walked right up to the men, parting Hulk and Beanpole like Moses parting the sea. He looked from one to the other, then over to Yellow Hair before returning his gaze to the men.

"This ain't PROSTAFF. You get out of hand, and we take care of the problem." Manny jabbed a thumb at his chest before pointing randomly out to the crowd and, Anthony realized, 187 closing in on the scene. "Now, I don't know *how* we're gonna go about solving the problem, but me and my boys like to get creative, and this here fish fry has us feeling inspired."

Manny crossed his arms and smiled from one side of his face to the other.

Then Yellow Hair, Hulk, and Beanpole all scurried away.

Anthony turned to Renee with his hand raised, ready

to throw a high-five. Her palm was already waiting. Their hands slapped, and then she kissed him full on the mouth.

"Check it out," Anthony said as they parted, nodding at an unlikely duo — or not so unlikely — chatting over two heaping plates: fish and coleslaw for the county commissioner; crawfish, shrimp etouffee, and boudin for Eddison Fisher himself.

"Don't get mad." Renee rubbed him on the shoulder.

"I'm not mad at all." An emotional exhale to realize the truth as he said it. "I'm glad he's seeing our neighborhood at its best."

Eddison glanced over, saw Anthony looking, and gave him a genuine smile.

Anthony smiled back, meaning it.

Fisher said something to the commissioner, then both men came walking over.

Renee said, "Be nice."

"I'm always nice."

Then Eddison was in front of them, clapping Anthony on the back. "Thank you so much for doing this." Another smile. He pushed the glasses up on the bridge of his nose with a laugh. "My grandmother was from Louisiana, and I've been tasting things today that I've not had the joy of tasting since I was a boy."

For a moment, it was like the rain going dry and the sun breaking into the sky that morning. In that flicker, Anthony allowed himself to believe in a miracle. "Does this mean that you're going to give up the development?"

"Of course not." Eddison shook his head while giving Anthony a kind smile he would have surely seen as condescending just a few weeks before. "You can't stop progress, son. What's happening here will happen with or without me. But I'll do everything in my power to make sure the development moves this neighborhood forward. Now, if you'll excuse me, I do believe that some more shrimp etouffee is calling my name."

"Enjoy the food, and thank you for coming," said Renee.

"Yes, thank you for coming." And again, Anthony meant it.

The commissioner turned to Anthony once Eddison left, then he looked dramatically around. "There are at least a dozen city violations happening right now, but I'm going to look the other way. This is—"

He stopped, pivoting away from the conversation to watch Troy frog-marching someone out of the party.

The commissioner cleared his throat. "As I was saying, this is a great event, all things considered." He looked around again, but this time the gesture was appreciative more than performative. "Something about this has really captured the city's imagination."

Anthony smiled. "Things usually go better when I do them like my Grandmoh would have."

"You sound like a wise man." The commissioner returned Anthony's smile. "Have you ever thought about running events professionally? And would you ever consider doing something sanctioned by the city next time?"

"Not only have I thought about it," Anthony nodded, although the thought had never crossed his mind, "I was born for the job. But I'll have to check in with my … business partner, Kevin, to make sure we want to take on the city as a client."

"Fair enough." The commissioner reached into his pocket, withdrew his wallet, then pulled out a card and handed it to Anthony. "And it will have to have a lot more structure than this party. I should probably get out of here before someone catches me allowing alcohol to be sold without a license."

Renee looked like she might want to shower Anthony with praise, and he was a fan of that happening, but Michael came over just as the commissioner was walking away.

"Johnny Law trying to bring you down?" Michael cast a suspicious glance at the commissioner. "We need to close shop? Columbo going for reinforcements?"

"Columbo was a detective, not a bureaucrat." Anthony laughed. "I think I might've just BS'd my way into some business with the city."

"No shit?" Michael looked back at Anthony in a blend of awe and disbelief.

"I know, right?" Renee said, still beaming beside him. "*My* man!"

"You always could tell a good story. I'm so proud of you, cuz." Michael pulled him into a hug, then yanked him back when Anthony tried to pull away, believing the moment was over.

After a lingering pause, Michael finally let him go. "And on that note, it looks like this is a new chapter for both of us ... I'll be heading off tomorrow. A group I know is learning sheep herding in New Zealand."

"*New Zealand*," Anthony repeated. "Isn't that where you said Lacy was headed?"

"She might be part of the group," Michael smirked.

"Interesting," nodded Renee.

Anthony put a hand on Michael's shoulder. "You know you're welcome to stay as long as you want to."

"Of course. But why would I want to do that? You're the storyteller. DOESN'T THIS FEEL LIKE THE

CLIMAX TO YOU?" Michael dramatically yelled over a boisterous explosion of music, gesturing at a neighborhood pickled in joy.

Then, as if God Himself was helping Michael prove his point, a police helicopter came swooping through the sky before it was suddenly *thwapping* directly overhead.

"What the—" Renee stopped as Kevin ran toward them, screaming his explanation while laughing.

"CARS ARE BACKED UP ON THE FREEWAY!"

Then a report from Rob, bellowing even louder. "THERE'S A MASSIVE TRAFFIC JAM ON ALL SIDES!"

Anthony, Renee, and Michael all blurted in unison: "WE FORGOT ABOUT PARKING!"

"I can't believe it." Anthony slapped his forehead. "I sure as hell can't be making that kind of mistake if I'm working for the city. At least the commissioner already left."

"Dumbass." Michael laughed. "You don't think he'll hear about this?"

"Or see it on the news?" Kevin pointed to a second helicopter, this one from WGCL-TV.

Anthony couldn't believe what he was seeing ... or feeling ... or thinking. Everything was so perfectly in and out of control.

He erupted in laughter. A current of pure emotion, born as a chuckle before bursting into a tsunami of unrestrained delight. His appreciation rang through the air, hitting the crowd around him in lingering, heaving guffaws.

Friends and neighbors joined him, followed by guests, until a chorus of laughter rolled through the cul-de-sac with newcomers joining in, even though by the end, few of them even knew why.

When Down in the Treme struck the first notes of "Do What You Wanna," Anthony did what he most wanted to do. Swung Renee into dancing the Second Line. Riley and Rob joined them, then Joy Jones and Darius. Finally, even Wendall and Miss Adelaide were getting down in the street.

The dance soon became a soul train of a magnitude Anthony had never witnessed before. He looked up at the pair of helicopters, wondering what the party looked like from up there. From down here, it felt like perfection.

Just then, the DJ screamed into the microphone, "Everybody get your hands up — *we're on TV!*" Everyone waved their hands towards the hovering helicopters from left to right, in perfect sync with the music.

As the fish fry rolled into its closing, the tribe of neighbors who had become friends gathered in a teeming mass of green and purple shirts, looking around in awe at this beautiful thing they created. Down in the Treme had just concluded their second encore, and DJ Donkey was now taking over.

The food was all gone, but drinks were still coming. The neighbors stayed silent as they watched the multitude mingle, a handful still dancing with more sitting on the grass, porches, and even the street, rubbing full bellies and enjoying great conversation.

"This turned out to be a pretty good neighborhood." Miss Adelaide broke their silence with a question for the group. "Where do you suppose we'll all end up next?

Anthony suddenly felt like the leader, and maybe that was long overdue. He assumed the duty of answering first. "I don't know where we'll all be soon, but I'm sure we'll find a way to fry together. And I can hardly wait to see what happens the next time we do."

"What are the odds that there will be some more of

that?" Michael pointed to the cameraman and reporter from WGCL-TV.

It was all so picture-perfect, even before the fireworks started.

"I'll be right back," Renee whispered, leaning in to kiss Anthony on his cheek.

"*Now?* But you'll miss the fireworks."

"I'll just be a minute!" Then she scampered away.

He knew she was up to something and couldn't wait to see what it was.

Anthony sat on their lawn, palms flat on the grass, staring up at the sky when Renee returned and settled down beside him.

"I'm really going to miss this neighborhood," he said.

"Me too. But I bet you anything that we're really going to love the next one. And seriously, could we have hoped for a better goodbye?"

An explosion punctuated the end of her thought with a sizzling shower of pink and yellow sparks in the sky, raining like glitter from the darkness.

"No way." Anthony shook his head.

"I got you a present." She held out a box.

He took the gift into his hands, heart pounding from the thought of what he knew it probably was. The size, the shape, and the weight made a promise, then the box under the wrapping paper kept it.

"I really needed a new laptop." Anthony looked up at her in pure appreciation.

"It's not just any laptop. It's the computer you'll use to start telling your stories. That's always been your dream, Anthony. Your job at ContentHive is gone, but now so are your excuses."

"I'm not making excuses ... I just need to figure out what I should write about."

Renee looked around, then leaned in and kissed him on the cheek again.

Then she whispered, "Maybe you can write about this."

Epilogue

FIVE YEARS LATER ...

"Are you planning on driving around until you run out of gas?" Renee asked, smacking Anthony playfully on his arm.

"We've been driving for less than ten minutes," he replied with a laugh. "And don't act like you don't know where we're going."

"Are we almost there, Daddy?" Ivy chirped from the backseat.

"Almost there." Anthony nodded, catching Bria's curious eyes in the rearview and giving her a smile.

"I want to watch *The Princess and the Frog*."

"We can all watch it together when we get home," Anthony said. "Again ..."

Renee turned around to address their four-year-old daughter. "You know how much Daddy loves watching *The Princess and the Frog* with you. He just wants to show us something, then we'll go home."

"What do you want to show us, Daddy?"

"Where you came from." A simple answer that Anthony had been pondering a while.

Ivy asked another hundred questions or so — in the last half-year she'd barely stopped — before he was finally swinging his now-ancient Wrangler onto Edgewood, which now looked like another world from the one where he and Renee had started their new life together.

"That's where your mom and I used to live before you were born." Anthony pointed to a home that was no longer there, looking back into the rearview to see Ivy's reaction.

"It's so big!" she squealed.

"Daddy is trying to say that we used to live in a house right over there, before that house was torn down and they built the apartment building."

"Why did they tear it down?" Ivy asked.

"Because you can't stop progress," Anthony replied, without a note of bitterness in his laugh.

The old neighborhood was definitely gone, but contrary to what Anthony had imagined would eventually happen once Eddison Fisher got his way, the neighborhood did appear to be thriving. Edgewood had been turned into an area for living, working, and playing.

Anthony wondered — same as he always did when he found himself in their old cul-de-sac, after curiosity inspired a drive to revisit his personal history — what life would have been like if the developer hadn't gotten his way. Would they have been just as happy bringing Ivy into the world here, or could the perfection they'd found on the other side of the city only be discovered once they were willing to shed the life of an old skin and leave it behind?

Five years ago Anthony believed that his dream and Eddison Fisher's were at odds, but now he understood that one fantasy could always beget another. Without the developer digging into his dreams, Anthony wouldn't have unearthed his own.

"The park is pretty," Ivy said.

"It sure is," Renee agreed.

"I like it!" declared their daughter with an affirmative nod.

"Me too." Anthony loved that he wasn't lying. "See that place over there?"

He pointed to where Eddison Fisher's presentation from the now-infamous municipal meeting had placed a Starbucks, but the corner was still void of the coffee shop, boasting a new and improved version of a neighborhood classic instead. Still The Canopy, the place was now twice its old size, and without having lost a drop of the soul that Darius Jones had filled the original with. One side of The Canopy now had a thriving bakery — even in early afternoon there was still a line out the door — while the other side boasted a giant sign that read Canopy Music and delivered on its promise.

Ivy nodded. "Is that a store?"

"It sure is," Anthony told her. "But it's also a place to hang out with friends and listen to some really great music."

Keith Jones had talked Eddison Fisher into championing the expansion of The Canopy and giving his company a fair shot at running the whole place. He now did everything with it that his old man had always wanted to, and more, but with a team of people working side by side. They were serving a blended group of residents while building a business that had already been written up in the local press an enviable number of times. He proudly displayed the best of those articles, matted, framed, and hung behind the bar on the more musical side of his enterprise. Keith was thrilled to be living his dream while his folks were living theirs with a small condo in West Midtown and the occasional trip, including two jaunts to Belize in the last three years.

"Are we going to the store for music?" Ivy asked.

"Not now, but I'd love to come back later if you want to."

"Are we going to play at the park?"

"We need to get home," Renee prompted Anthony while speaking to Ivy. "Your Uncle Michael is waiting for us."

"Just a few minutes," Anthony said, grinning at Renee to encourage her agreement.

"Just a few minutes," Renee repeated with a smile.

"YAY!" Ivy exclaimed from the back.

After fifteen minutes of furious play at the splash pad in the pristine park, that both parents agreed Bria would be remembering for a while, they got back in the car and drove for twenty minutes to their small house with its tidy yard, backing up to a sprawling park that wasn't anywhere as new or admittedly nice as the one over near Edgewood, but the trees were older and thus the roots were deeper. Ivy loved it (she had named the place Smoothie Park and listed it as her "second best friend") and her parents had never felt prouder.

The home was theirs and they loved every square inch, if not forever then with all of their hearts right now.

"Are we late to the fish fry?" Ivy asked.

Anthony swung onto Vinings Drive while shaking his head. "Looks like it's just getting started."

They could see a collection of familiar faces already occupying their side yard. Kevin and Jonah were fighting over who would get to operate the fryer. It was a regular argument. Kevin swore that he knew more about it because he was a co-owner of the now city-famous Fish

Fry event company. Jonah argued that Kevin was a figure-head only. Ezekiel and Wendall seemed content to watch others argue for once.

There were some notable missing faces. Joy and Darius were off on another cruise and the other bros had moved to different parts of the country. And of course, Miss Adelaide had never left Edgewood, passing away gracefully in her sleep just days before she was due to move out. They always made sure to raise a glass to her at their annual fry. But Lacy was there, tuning her guitar, which meant they should see …

"UNCLE MICHAEL!" Ivy ran over to where Michael was sitting on the front porch petting Fry Guy and jumped into his arms.

Fry Guy leaped up and planted his front paws on Ivy's back to lick her, not wanting to be omitted from the reunion.

"You know you could have waited inside," said Renee.

"I wanted him to see me waiting." Michael nodded at Anthony, then turned to Ivy. "Riley and Rob are inside prepping the Jell-O shots." He leaned down and whispered a secret. "I think they might have a present."

"Will you come with me, Mommy?" Knowing the answer, she held out her hand.

Renee took it, smiled at the boys, then trotted toward the rollicking fry to find her friends. "Good luck," she said with a glance back at Anthony.

"Why is she wishing you luck?" Michael asked.

"She knows how painful it is for me to keep pretending that I enjoy your company." Anthony opened his front door and gestured Michael inside. "Or maybe she knows about your IBS and how it affects me."

"Man, don't even joke about that. A moment in the

mouth followed by an hour on the shitter ..." He shook his head. "No thank you."

"Seriously ..." Anthony looked back at him, picking up a wrapped present from an end table by the sofa. "I wanted you to have this."

"Thanks, man." Michael accepted the gift with surprise, unwrapping the package and laughing as pieces of torn paper floated to the floor. He looked down at the cover, staring for a long second before looking back up at Anthony, blinking to keep his tears from falling. "You actually wrote a book?"

"I did." Anthony nodded.

Michael laughed again, now pointing at the cover. "And you called it Atlanta Fish Fry?"

"I'm sure you can guess what it's about."

"You know a person thinks highly of themselves when they give you something they wrote as a present." Michael made a face, like Anthony should be ashamed of himself.

"I do think highly of myself," Anthony agreed. "And I think highly of Renee and Ivy, and all of our family and friends. Including you. I think highly of all the people I spend my time with. That's why I spend my time with them. Life constantly changes, so home and family are where you make it."

"So if you're telling me all of your life lessons out loud then I'm guessing I don't have to actually read the book, right?"

Anthony shrugged. "I figured you'd be dying to see what I said about you."

"Did you say I was smart and funny and handsome?"

"I said you were short."

"Man, you know there ain't nothing a man can do about his height. I should—"

"You should what?" Renee asked from behind the open

door. She looked at the book and then at the boys. "Never mind. Who cares. It looks like you all are done in here, and the Edgewood gang is waiting."

"You the MC of this thing?" Michael asked.

"Something like that." Renee rolled her eyes.

Ivy ran up behind Mommy, then grabbed a leg and poked her head around it to look at her father. "Say it, Daddy!"

"No." He shook his head, laughing and knowing that of course he was going to.

"Please!"

"Can he say it outside?" Renee nodded back at the door.

"Say what?" Michael asked.

"Betty Botter bought some butter, but she said the butter's bitter. If I put it in my—"

"Anthony." Renee gave him a look.

"—batter, it will make my batter bitter. But—"

"Daddy!" Ivy giggled.

"—a bit of better butt—" Anthony stopped.

"Say what?" Michael asked again.

"Outside," Renee repeated.

Anthony laughed on his way to the door.

Once on the porch, with his giggling little girl wrapped around his knees, he said, "Life's a fish, and then you fry."

About the Author

Anthony 'AJ' Joiner is an entrepreneur, bestselling author, radio personality and founder of BLOOKSY.COM — the software platform that uses artificial intelligence to make writing simple. AJ built software for companies such as CDC, Delta Airlines, and Georgia Department of Transportation. Since leaving corporate America he has published over 250 authors and helped thousands more through start writing their books over the last five years.

His software Blooksy is being piloted in several universities, and hundreds of writers are now using it to write books.

He's been on the #1 drive-time radio show, The Willie Moore Jr. Show, is a passionate New Orleans Saints fan, and proudly represents the #1 HBCU in America – Southern University.

A native of Leesville, Louisiana, AJ loves nothing more than, eating authentic Louisiana food, and yelling WHODAT during football season. You can find out more about AJ by visiting: www.anthonyjoiner.com or @ajjoiner on Instagram (and if you're interested in writing a book, academic article, or white paper visit: www.blooksy.com)

CPSIA information can be obtained
at www.ICGtesting.com
Printed in the USA
BVHW070842200423
662716BV00016B/682

9 781629 552200